HANDSOME BOSS

Handsome Devils Book 2

LORI WILDE

LIZ ALVIN

❧ I ❧

Some men should never wear a shirt, Emma Montgomery decided as she watched Nathan Barrett shoot baskets on the sports court behind his house. The man was poetry in motion—a Shakespearian sonnet, a love poem by Keats.

He spun toward her, and her gaze skittered down his muscled chest again.

Or maybe a really naughty limerick.

Yep, he was a handsome devil alright.

"You wait here," Leigh Barrett said from the passenger seat of Emma's compact car. "I need to talk to Nathan for a second."

Now that didn't sound good. Not good at all. Emma pulled her gaze away from Nathan and looked at his sister.

"You assured me that everything was set," Emma pointed out.

Leigh bobbed her head, her short black hair brushing against her chin. "It is set, so stop worrying."

Not in the least reassured, Emma asked, "Nathan knows I'm coming, right?"

Again, the head bob. "You bet."

"And he agreed that I could have the technical writing job?"

"Yep, that, too."

Still unable to shake the feeling that she'd stepped off the side of a mountain and was about to take one heck of a plunge, Emma pressed on. "And he did agree that I could use his garage apartment this summer, right?"

"Everything is fine." Leigh shoved open the door to the car. "You're such a worrier, Emma. No wonder you live on antacids. You need to relax. Take a few deep breaths. Find your center."

"My what?"

"You know. The child within. Your feminine side." With a grin, she added, "Feng shui yourself."

Emma laughed and felt the tension level inside her slip down a notch or two. She should have known when push came to shove, Leigh wouldn't let her down. She knew how much Emma needed this summer job.

"I promise to relax if you're certain everything is fine."

Leigh rolled her eyes. "Say it slowly with me: Ev...er...y thi...ng is fi...ne."

Emma smiled. "Everything is fine."

Leigh glanced at her brother, then back at Emma. "Very good. Now give me a head start. I just need to clarify one tiny detail with Nathan, then we can get you moved into the garage apartment."

There was something in the way Leigh said the

words "one tiny detail" that made the feeling of dread rush right back into Emma's stomach and settle down for a long stay. Something was rotten in Denmark, or rather in Honey, Texas. This small town might call itself the "sweetest town in Texas," but right now, she had the distinct feeling that everything wasn't "sweet."

Emma didn't want to ask. Not at all. Intuitively, she knew she wasn't going to like the answer. But she had to know, so squinting in an attempt to lessen the expected blow, she asked, "What detail do you need to clarify with Nathan?"

"Oh, nothing special," Leigh said. "I just need to mention a few things." She swung her legs out of the car, then said in a rush, "Like that you're going to work for him at his software company for the summer while you live in the apartment over his garage. No biggie."

Emma's mouth dropped open, but before she could say a word, Leigh sprinted away from the car. No biggie? This was a really big biggie. Nathan Barrett knew absolutely nothing about her plans.

Good grief. Fumbling in her purse, Emma tugged out her roll of antacids and tossed a couple into her mouth. The familiar chalky taste brought her a tiny degree of comfort.

"You can do this," she muttered, willing the butter-flies—no, make that condors—thrashing around in her stomach to chill. "You can handle this."

Even though she only half believed herself, she climbed out of her car. Leigh was already on the basket-ball court, talking with her brother.

"Darn her," Emma muttered, slamming her car door. She should have known better than to trust her summer plans to Leigh Barrett. Leigh was funny and full of life and great to be around, but she was also kooky, and crazy, and often unreliable.

The last character trait was the one Emma should have focused on when Leigh had brought up this idea about coming to Honey. She should have checked and double-checked these plans like a bride planning a flaw-less wedding.

But she hadn't questioned a thing.

"You coward," she muttered to herself as she reached the outer corner of the sports court. She hadn't questioned Leigh simply because her friend had promised the solution to all her problems. Leigh had assured Emma that her brother needed a technical writer for the summer and that the pay would be great. And when Emma had mentioned she'd need a place to stay, Leigh had had the answer to that one, too. Nathan had a nice apartment over his three-car garage.

What could be better? She'd be able to work on her dissertation in the evenings after she came home from Barrett Software. And she'd pick up some nice change to pay the never-ending college bills.

What a dummy. She might as well tattoo the word sap on her forehead. Just because she'd wanted this job to work out wasn't an excuse not to check her facts before leaving Austin and driving to Honey with Leigh. Her super-organized father would be appalled that she hadn't verified the plans.

At the moment, jobless and homeless, she was pretty appalled, too.

As she approached Leigh and her brother, she heard Leigh hastily explaining the situation while Nathan frowned. The man wasn't pleased. That much was obvious. He glanced in Emma's direction, then walked over and grabbed a T-shirt off a bench and pulled it on.

"It's no big deal," Leigh was saying as Emma drew even with them.

"It's a very big deal," Nathan shot back. He turned and looked at Emma. "Hello."

Wow. Nathan was even better-looking close up. Every female hormone in Emma's body sat up and took notice, and for the briefest of moments, Emma forgot her jobless/homeless problem and simply enjoyed looking at him.

"Nathan, this is my friend, Emma Montgomery," Leigh said. "Emma, this is Nathan, who will help me out, or I'll tell all of his secrets."

Nathan glanced at his sister. "What secrets? I don't have any secrets."

Leigh snorted, an unladylike sound that oddly fit her personality. "Oh, please, sell it to someone who's never met you. I know all the good things. Like that you cried for an hour the first time a girl kissed you—"

Nathan frowned. "I was six."

"Or the time when you had a crush on Lindsey Franklin, so you kept calling her up, but when she'd answer, you'd hang up—"

"I was eleven."

Leigh put her hands on her hips and said, "Best of all, how about the time in high school when MaryLou Delacourte's parents thought she was at a slumber party when actually she was with you, and you two were—"

"Stop." Nathan tipped his head and looked at Emma, humor gleaming in his amazing blue eyes.

Despite being annoyed at his sister, there was a healthy dose of brotherly love obvious in his treatment of Leigh. He might not be happy with what she'd done, but he was being an exceptionally good sport about it. "Do you have any objections to being a material witness to a crime?"

Emma laughed. "Under the circumstances, I completely understand."

"Ha ha. Like you'd ever do anything to me." Leigh leaned up and gave her brother a loud, smacking kiss on his cheek. "Jeez, you're sweaty."

"I was shooting hoops and not expecting company," he said. His gaze returned to Emma. "Sorry."

"I'm the one who's sorry. I had no idea this wasn't arranged." She frowned at Leigh. "I was under the impression you knew all about the plans. I guess I should head on back to Austin."

"Nathan Eric Barrett, how rude can you be?" Leigh scolded. "Look what you did."

"What I did? I haven't done anything to anyone," he said calmly. "Go inside, Leigh. I want to talk to Emma alone."

"But if I'm not here—"

"Go inside," Nathan repeated.

Finally, muttering and fussing the whole way, Leigh headed across the sports court and disappeared inside the large brick house.

Left alone with Nathan, Emma tried to keep her gaze firmly tacked on his face. Boy oh boy, it wasn't easy. His T-shirt hugged his muscles, but since she hated it when men talked to her chest, she imagined Nathan would hate it if she had a conversation with his pecs.

"So, if I'm following this, Leigh told you I had a job opening for a technical writer at Barrett Software," Nathan said.

Emma nodded, hoping against hope that at least a little bit of Leigh's story had been true. She crossed her fingers. "Do you?"

His expression was kind. "I'm sorry, no."

"Oh." She swallowed past the nervous lump in her throat and struggled to maintain control. *Breathe, Emma. Breathe.*

She fumbled in her pocket, searching for her antacids, then remembered they were in her purse. That was okay. She could handle this. Sure, there weren't a lot of really great jobs lying around that would only last the summer. And sure, she'd been counting on this job to help pay off some bills. But she could manage. She hadn't made it all the way to the doctoral program at the University of Texas without becoming a pro at dealing with problems. This was only a setback. A big setback, granted, but one she could handle.

"I see," she managed to say when Nathan continued to give her a sympathetic look.

"I understand that Leigh also promised you could live in the apartment above my garage." This time it was a statement, not a question.

The feeling of dread she'd been experiencing now took on monumental proportions. "Let me guess, you don't have an apartment over your garage, either."

"Yes, I do."

She nodded. "Of course you—you do?" Blinking, she tried to decide what that meant. Could this possibly be a tiny streak of good luck struggling to shine through the dark cloud?

"Yes, but it's my storage room, filled with old junk. Not really suitable to live in at the moment." Ah, heck. Emma blew out an exasperated breath. Great. Just great No job. No place to live. Talk about with friends like Leigh, who needed enemies.

"Well, that's that. I guess I'd better go. Thank you for your time," she said.

Nathan grinned. "You give up too easily." He tossed her the basketball, which she just managed to catch. "Do you play?"

She looked at the ball in her hands. "What?"

"Sink it."

With a shrug, she turned, assessed her shot, and neatly sunk the ball. When she turned back to look at Nathan, he nodded.

"Nice shot."

"I played in high school," she told him. "Look, why don't I say goodbye to Leigh and head back—"

"Wait." Nathan wandered over and picked up the basketball. He dribbled it as he came back over to stand next to her. She tried, really she did, to keep from staring at him, but how much was a woman supposed to resist? The man was gorgeous, absolutely gorgeous, and despite the disappointment flooding through her at the moment, she wasn't dead.

"Do you know why I sent Leigh inside?" he asked, a roguish gleam in his eyes.

Emma considered the possibilities, finally settling on the most obvious. "Because you were afraid you'd do something terrible to her if you didn't?"

He chuckled, the sound warm and rich and electrifying as it danced across Emma's skin. This man was like fudge ripple ice cream. Much, much too tempting.

"I sent Leigh inside so she could sweat for a little while. Even without looking, I know she's watching us through the kitchen window, wondering what we're talking about."

Emma glanced toward the house and caught a glimpse of Leigh peering through the window before she disappeared. "You're right. She's there."

Nathan smiled. "I know. See, she's about ninety-nine percent sure I'll save her. I always have in the past. But there's that one percent of uncertainty, the tiniest fragment of doubt, that's making her climb the walls. I figure the least I can do is make her squirm for a few minutes before I save her."

Emma snagged on to what he'd said. He'd save Leigh? Did that mean she would get a job and a place to stay after all? Was it too soon to yell yahoo and dance around with joy?

She studied Nathan and tried not to let her optimism run away with her, but she couldn't help asking, "Are you saying you do have a job?"

"A couple. Neither of them is for a technical writer, though." His gaze skimmed her casual outfit of jean shorts and a green T-shirt, then nodded toward the basketball. "Want to try to make that shot again?"

At this point, Emma would do just about anything to get a job. She didn't have time to waste going back to Austin and seeing if she could scrounge up something at the university. "Sure."

He tossed her the ball, and she sunk it.

"You're good." For a second, he studied her, and Emma's pulse rate picked up. As much as she'd like to attribute the metabolic change to being nervous, she knew that was bunk. Her heart was racing because she was attracted to Nathan. Very attracted.

"Tell me about yourself," Nathan said.

This was hardly the place she would have picked for an interview, but at this point, she was willing to be interviewed in the middle of Interstate 20 if it meant she could get a job.

"I'm working on my doctorate in English at the University of Texas," she told him.

"That's where you met Leigh."

"Yes." She glanced toward the house, then added, "And up until a few minutes ago, we were great friends."

Nathan laughed again, and Emma had to admit, that was a sound she could get used to without any trouble. "It's not that bad. Things will work out. My brothers and I are used to doing damage control when necessary to pull Leigh out of the fire."

"That doesn't upset you?"

Nathan snagged the ball again and easily made a shot. "Don't get me wrong. I don't approve of Leigh's methods. But she's just that way. Always has been. It's part of her personality...part of her charm."

"Being devious and conniving?"

His grin was devilish. "Yes. You'll get used to it."

Emma sincerely doubted that. "Does that devious streak run in your family?"

Nathan's smile was oh-so enticing. "Me? I'm completely harmless."

Yeah, right, and she could wrestle crocodiles.

※

THIS TIME, LEIGH HAD REALLY TAKEN THE CAKE. Nathan glanced at the house and wondered not for the first time how pure mischief could flow through his sister's veins. Even for her, this was a bit much. Not only was she yanking him around, but she was also embroiling one of her friends in whatever this latest scheme was. A friend who was obviously upset.

He'd bet his new car that Leigh's motives were far from pure. If he had to guess, he'd bet his sister was up to something.

Leigh was always up to something.

And it didn't take a rocket scientist to figure out what. The data was pretty clear. Leigh had arranged for Emma Montgomery to not only spend the summer working at Barrett Software, but she'd also managed to have Emma living at his house. Emma, who just so happened to be smart and gorgeous—two traits he greatly admired in a woman, which Leigh knew. Could his sister be trying to fix him up? He knew she was tired of him interfering in her life. But tired enough that she'd go this far?

The concept was almost too diabolical to entertain. That would mean Leigh was willing to use her friend Emma as bait. Could Leigh actually be that sneaky?

He sighed. Of course, she could. He knew for a fact that she'd meddled in their brother Chase's life, fixing him up with the town librarian. Sure, Chase and Megan made a great couple, but he didn't want to be fixed up, especially not by Leigh.

He glanced back at Emma. Did she realize she was a

victim? Did she know her friend was setting her up? He wasn't picking up any flirtatious vibes from her, so he was fairly certain she truly was here simply for a job.

But when she smiled at him, Nathan felt his heart rate rev. She really was gorgeous.

"Think we should stretch this out a little longer and make Leigh squirm some more?" he asked.

Emma nodded. "Absolutely. Squirming is good for her."

Nathan couldn't help pointing out, "I see a little deviousness runs in your family, too."

"Apparently."

He looked at his house. Leigh stood at the kitchen window, watching them.

She was guilty all right.

He turned his attention back to Emma. She had wavy auburn hair that hung to her shoulders. Auburn hair was his personal favorite. Or rather, it had become his favorite in the past few minutes. Emma also had his favorite color eyes—hazel. Again, his propensity for hazel eyes was a recent discovery, but still, he really liked that shade. A lot.

Eyes like Emma Montgomery's seemed to change color every few minutes. At the moment, they were a steely gray—sharp, intense, not missing a thing.

The back door to the house flew open and banged against the outside wall.

"I can't take it anymore, Nathan," Leigh hollered from the open door to the kitchen. "I swear if you send Emma home, you'll no longer be my favorite brother."

Nathan grinned and winked at Emma. "Is that a promise?"

"Ha ha. Now stop tormenting us and help unpack Emma's car. You two have to go to work tomorrow. You can't stand around here all day yammering on the basketball court." Without waiting for his response, Leigh headed over to the small yellow compact car parked in his driveway.

"Guess she told us," Nathan said, waiting for Emma to precede him to her car.

"You know, we don't have to do what she says," Emma pointed out. "I mean, you don't have to give me a job...if you really don't want to."

Nathan knew that. Just because Leigh might have concocted some sort of scheme didn't mean he was going to fall for it. Oh sure, he'd let Emma work at Barrett Software. He'd even let her live in the apartment once they got it straightened up. But that was all. He wasn't going to fall for Emma Montgomery, no matter how hard his sister tried.

"It's no problem, Emma," he assured her. "We'll work something out."

Feeling more in control of the situation, he headed toward the car to help. "Hey, Leigh, hold up. The garage apartment is full of junk. Emma will have to stay in the house for a couple of nights."

Emma had been walking along next to him, but now she stopped.

"I'm turning into a real inconvenience," she said. "I feel terrible about this."

They were close enough for Leigh to hear them, and his sister answered before he had the chance.

"Emma, stop being so polite to Nathan. It will make him think even higher of himself than he does already, and none of us wants that. The whole town adores him. Everyone goes gaga over him, so don't puff up his ego anymore, or he's apt to float away."

Nathan nudged his sister. "Hey, remember, kiddo, I'm helping you out. Don't bite the hand that's saving your tush."

She rolled her eyes at him, looking more like a six-year-old than a young woman about to graduate from college.

"You know I love you," she said. "But you also have more than your fair share of self-confidence. You don't need Emma telling you how great you are." She fluttered her eyelashes. "You've got the ladies of Honey to do that."

Emma gave him an inquisitive look. "You do?"

Before Nathan could make even a token effort to rescue his reputation, Leigh jumped back in.

"All the ladies in town are besotted with my brother. They chase him relentlessly."

"No, they don't. Not exactly." He ruffled his sister's hair and grabbed a couple of suitcases out of the car.

Leigh turned to Emma. "Trust me. That's exactly what they do. They. Chase. Him."

Nathan shook his head and headed toward the kitchen. There was no sense wasting his breath fighting with Leigh. When she got going, there was nothing to do but hang on for the ride. He could hear the women talking as they followed behind him. His sister discussing him was never a good thing, so he decided to change the subject.

"Emma, you sure you don't want to take the summer

off?" Nathan asked. "You could laze around on a beach somewhere."

"I really do need a job this summer. If you don't think—"

"Nathan, you're upsetting Emma," Leigh said. "Stop being rude and assure her that you have a job."

"I already told her I'd work something out." He set down the suitcases and stared at his sister. "In case you've forgotten, up until ten minutes ago, I didn't know you intended on bringing someone home with you. All you told me on the phone last night was that you'd caught a ride with a friend."

If he'd expected Leigh to look contrite, he would have been disappointed. She glared at him.

"Get over that, Nathan. Jeez. It's like ancient history. So I surprised you. Big woo. Now accept that Emma is here and give her a job."

"Leigh, do you always push your brother around like this?" Emma asked.

Nathan pinned Leigh with a direct look. "Yes. She does."

"Oh, you poor baby. I'm so mean to you." Leigh leaned over and gave him another kiss on the cheek. "You adore me, and you know it. If it weren't for me livening up your life, you'd fall into a big pile of computer code and never come out. Admit it—you've been bored while I've been at college, haven't you?"

He pretended to consider her question. "Bored? Have I been bored? My life has been restful while you've been gone."

"Your life will be restful when you're dead, too, but that doesn't make it a good thing."

Nathan laughed. Truthfully, he was glad Leigh was home. Sure, she was a pain at times, but she also was a lot of fun.

"One of these days, I'm going to move and not give you the forwarding address," he teased as he picked up the suitcases and headed inside the house.

"Won't happen. Now figure out what you're going to do to help Emma."

As he led the way inside the house, he debated which of the two open jobs to offer Emma. One was in personnel, and Emma struck him as the type who would be good with people. The other job was as his assistant. His current assistant was on maternity leave, and he was desperate.

"My assistant just had a baby, and I need someone to fill in for the summer. Barrett Software is working on an easily customized accounting package for small businesses that we're going to demo in Dallas in six weeks at BizExpo, one of the biggest tech shows in the country. The time frame is kind of tight, and the program still has some problems, but if we make it, we'll get a lot of publicity. I really need help keeping everything moving. Sound like something you could do?"

"Of course, Emma can do it," Leigh said with a huff. "She's amazing. Unbelievable. Incredible."

Emma sighed. "Leigh, so help me, if you say I can leap tall buildings in a single bound, I'm heading back to Austin."

"Har-de-har-har," Leigh said. "You two are just a couple of comedians. Here I've gone to all this trouble to help both of you, and you don't even seem to appreciate what I've done."

Nathan winked at Emma. "Do you believe this? She's playing the martyr."

"Doing it well, too," Emma said.

Nathan smiled at her, liking the auburn-haired beauty more and more. He was still looking at Emma when Leigh snorted.

"Fine. Laugh all you want. But there's going to come a day when both of you will thank me for this. Trust me." With that, Leigh flounced up the stairs, carrying one of Emma's suitcases with her.

Emma had come to stand next to him. She smelled like flowers—rich, luxurious flowers, probably due to her shampoo rather than any perfume. The scent was too unintentional to be perfume.

But something about that scent tantalized him more than any expensive perfume ever could.

"Was that a promise or a threat?" Emma asked.

"Sometimes with Leigh, it's hard to tell the difference," he admitted.

$\mathscr{H}$ 2 $\mathscr{H}$

"**W**ant to come to the movies with me tonight? It won't be any fun, but I guess you can come if you really want to," Leigh said from the doorway.

Emma looked at her friend, who showed about as much enthusiasm as a dental patient right before a root canal. "Are you sure you want me to come? You don't seem too happy about the idea."

Leigh leaned against the doorjamb. "Like I said, it won't be fun. In fact, it will bore you to death, and you'll probably end up being mad at me for bringing you. But if you truly, truly want to come along, then it's okay with me."

Emma laughed. "Wow, Leigh, that's truly one heck of an invitation."

A smile lurked around Leigh's mouth. "Yeah, I know. It truly sucked. And I don't mean it that way. You're my friend. I like spending time with you. I'm thrilled you're here."

Emma sat on the comfy, queen-size bed in Nathan's guest room. Just from looking at Leigh, she could tell the younger woman was plotting and planning. Funny how she'd never noticed this side of her friend before, but Leigh did indeed have a wide devious streak in her makeup.

"What movie are you going to see?" Emma asked, knowing she wasn't actually being invited along. But she couldn't help wishing the invitation were sincere. It would be fun to get out for a while and see the town. Nathan had headed into his office an hour ago, and frankly, Emma would feel weird wandering around the man's house alone. After all, they had just met this afternoon.

Leigh broke eye contact and shrugged. "I'm not really sure. Something gross and gory."

Emma laughed. "If the movie is gross, then why are you going?"

"My friend likes that sort of thing."

The pieces of this puzzle weren't fitting. "I thought you told Nathan you were going to the movies with someone named Sara," Emma said. "Sara likes gory, gross movies?"

Leigh's attention fixed on the drapes behind Emma. "Yeah, she's strange that way. But I know that's not the sort of thing you like, so my feelings won't be hurt if you say no."

By now, Emma no more believed Leigh was going to the movies with a girlfriend named Sara than she believed in Santa Claus. She took a couple of T-shirts from her suitcase and put them in the dresser drawer.

Then she faced Leigh. "Fess up, who are you going to the movies with? It's a guy, isn't it?"

It took a second or two, but finally Leigh laughed. "How did you possibly guess?"

"How could I possibly not guess? A rock could have figured out what you're up to. You're a terrible actress," Emma pointed out.

"Nathan believed me."

Emma didn't think so. Nathan had raised one eyebrow and looked more than a little amused when Leigh had told him of her plans. But all he'd said was that Leigh should bring Emma along since she was her guest. No doubt he'd figured Emma's presence would put the kibosh on any romantic interlude Leigh had planned.

"What's his name?" Emma asked.

"Jared Kendrick. He's great. I've known him for years, but we've never gone out before. I heard he was in town, so I called and asked him out." Her expression turned pleading. "Will you be too miserable if I leave you here alone? I'm an awful person, but I really want to go out with Jared. The man is serious eye candy."

Emma laughed at Leigh's description. "Okay, so he's good-looking. But what kind of person is he?"

"A very good-looking person," Leigh said, then relented and added, "relax, he won't do anything that I don't want him to, if that's what you're asking. But there isn't much most women don't want Jared to do."

As much as she wanted to pretend to be shocked, Emma couldn't be so hypocritical. She was lusting after Nathan even though she'd only just met the man.

Although her instincts told her he was a good guy, she knew almost nothing about him.

"I have no interest in standing in the way of true love," Emma told Leigh. "Have a nice evening."

Leigh grinned. "Thanks, but it's not true love. Not at all. Tonight is about having fun."

"Should I tell Nathan you'll be home late?"

With a vehement shake of her head, Leigh said, "No. Don't say a word. You don't know how my brothers act. They watch me like hawks. If you hadn't been here, Nathan wouldn't have gone into the office. He would've stayed home and stared at me all night."

"I don't believe you," Emma said. "Nathan seems like a man who has better things to do than babysit you."

Leigh sighed and sat on the corner of the dresser. "You would think so, wouldn't you? You would think those bozos would accept that I'm grown up and leave me alone. But nooooo. My brothers drive me crazy. Okay, maybe not Chase. Not anymore. But Nathan and Trent still do."

"Why did Chase stop?"

Leigh patted her chest over her heart. "Chase fell madly in love. He got married a couple of weeks ago, and he's currently away on his honeymoon. That's why I'm staying with Nathan. Normally I stay with Chase when I'm home from school, but I don't want to be anywhere near Chase's house when he and his bride, Megan, return home."

Intrigued despite herself, Emma asked, "Why not? I'm sure they wouldn't mind having you around."

Leigh groaned. "Pu-lease, it's not them I'm worried

about. It's me. I can only take so much lovey- dovey stuff before I go into sugar overload. Plus, it gets embarrassing. Everywhere I go, the two of them are fooling around." She shuddered. "He's my brother. Ick."

Emma laughed. "I understand. So falling in love has put Chase out of the babysitter business. But Leigh, Nathan didn't seem too concerned about you going out tonight." She gave her friend a meaningful look. "Trust me, he didn't believe your story about Sara any more than I did. No one would believe your story."

"Yeah, well, he pretended to buy my story because he wanted to go into the office. You wait, when he gets home, the first thing he'll do is ask you if I went out with a guy. Then he'll get all huffy and macho and tell me off when I come home tonight." She grinned. "If I come home tonight."

Emma wasn't comfortable with lying. "If he asks me where you are, I'm going to tell him the truth. I won't cover for you."

"Don't worry. You won't have to. This town is like gossip central. The CIA should come here to study espionage. I swear, two minutes after anyone spots Jared and me together, bam! Nathan's phone will ring over at Barrett Software. You can't get away with anything in Honey. Nada. No one can. No wonder Trent rarely has to arrest anyone. Peer pressure keeps everyone in line. It's a terrible place to be when you have a burning desire to run amok."

Emma would have to take Leigh's word on that one. Although she'd lived in lots of places while growing up, none of the towns had been small. They'd been huge cities, like L.A. or New York or Houston. She'd never had a problem disappearing into the crowd. Even though Austin wasn't as big as L.A., it was a fairly big city. And the university was large, so she didn't stand out there, either. She had friends, but she'd never become the object of gossip just for going out on a date.

She couldn't help sympathizing with Leigh. Living in a fishbowl like Honey with overprotective brothers couldn't be easy.

"Why don't you just level with your brothers?" Emma suggested. "Tell them you don't like them meddling in your life. They love you, so I'm sure they'll take your feelings into consideration."

Leigh laughed, loud and long. "Emma, no offense, but you don't know doodly about brothers, especially Texas brothers. Those boys won't back off no matter what I say. I'm their baby sister. They feel it's their duty to protect me, whether I like it or not. To them, it's a matter of honor."

"That's sexist."

"Naw. Not really. I feel it's my duty to protect them, too. For instance, if one of them hooked up with some bimbo and looked like he might let his hormones lead him down the aisle, I'd have to step in."

As an only child, Emma simply couldn't relate. That kind of interference would bother her. A lot.

"Well, if you feel you can butt into their lives, then I guess you can't complain when they butt into yours," Emma said.

Leigh snorted. "If it was an emergency, I'd butt in. But not for any old reason in the world, which is what my brothers do. Butt in for absolutely no reason. Like my date tonight."

Emma nodded, finally understanding Leigh's point. "I see. Tonight's date is no reason for your brothers to be alarmed."

When she turned toward Leigh for confirmation of her theory, the younger woman was clearly aghast at what Emma had said.

"No reason? Yikes, I hope not. I've gone to a lot of trouble to go out with Jared. Shame on you for even suggesting such a thing."

Emma laughed. "Sorry. Didn't mean to jinx your plans."

"That's okay. Nothing can ruin tonight."

When the doorbell rang, Leigh grinned at Emma, her blue eyes dancing with excitement. "Wish me luck."

Although Emma wasn't really sure wishing Leigh luck under these circumstances was a good thing, she still complied. "Good luck."

"Thanks. And sorry to jump ship on your first night in town. But Nathan should be home pretty soon. Then you can go back to staring at him like he rode up on a white horse."

Emma felt like the air stuck in her throat. "What?"

Leigh raised one eyebrow, a gesture reminiscent of her brother. "I'm not the only one here who likes a little eye candy. Just keep in mind, Nathan's a natural charmer. Don't take him too seriously."

Before Emma could say anything, Leigh waved and slipped out of the bedroom. Emma wanted to sprint after her and tell her she was all wrong, but what would be the point? She had stared at Nathan like he was a bowl full of chocolate bonbons and she was on a diet. She definitely deserved Leigh's warning.

Not wanting to risk bumping into Leigh and her date, Emma took her time unpacking. She left most of what she'd brought in the suitcases on the chance she might be able to move into the garage apartment soon. Once she was done, she wandered around her room for a couple of minutes, until the silence in the house made her antsy.

Then she gathered up the research material she'd been reading and headed downstairs. The family room had caught her eye on the five-minute tour Leigh had given her of the place. With its cream leather furniture and paneled walls, the room tugged on Emma's aesthetic side. Entering, she couldn't help thinking the dark-blue throw pillows were the exact same shade as Nathan's eyes. Except Nathan's eyes were warm, and inviting, and... Oops. Enough of that. Emma curled up in one of the overstuffed chairs and refused to think any more about throw pillows and Nathan's eyes. She had work to do, so she settled down with her pile of research material.

And promptly found herself thinking about Nathan again. Okay, this time wasn't really her fault. From this vantage point, she could see the mantel was lined with family pictures. Even though she told herself not to, the pictures pulled at her like a tractor beam, and before she knew it, she walked over to study them.

Leigh was in almost all the shots, as were three men. In each photo, Nathan was smiling at the camera. His smile invited her to smile back. The other two men were undeniably his brothers. Although they were equally handsome, Emma couldn't stop looking at Nathan. There was something about him that made her mind almost shut down, something that made her want to get lost in his sexy smile and enticing gaze.

"Stop it," she muttered to herself, determined not to let Nathan distract her. She had a dissertation to write on the female character arc in nineteenth-century American literature. She wasn't going to waste time mooning over some man.

"The heck with you, Nathan Barrett," Emma said, deliberately turning her back on the pictures. She picked up her research papers and started reading. No way was she going to let a handsome devil like Nathan muddle her brain. She shot a triumphant glance at the photos on the mantel. "Your plan won't work."

"What plan would that be?"

NATHAN STOOD IN THE DOORWAY TO THE FAMILY room, watching Emma. She jumped and yelped a little when he spoke, obviously startled. How she hadn't known he was standing here was beyond him. He certainly hadn't tried to be quiet coming into the house.

But she had been surprised. Really surprised. She currently sat with one hand over her heart, her wide hazel eyes staring at him.

"Where in the world did you come from?" Her voice had a breathless overtone to it that he found very appealing.

Hoping to lighten the mood, he said, "My parents told me they found me under a cabbage leaf, but I never believed them." He wandered into the room and sat on the sofa facing her. "What do you think? Sounds like a suspicious story, doesn't it? I mean, I could understand if they'd found me in a haystack. Or maybe in a basket left on the doorstep by a stork. But come on? A cabbage patch seems a bit implausible."

Emma was still staring at him, and as Nathan watched, a pale flush colored her pretty face. Now that was interesting. He'd love to know what had caused her to have that reaction.

"Where's Leigh?" he asked, already knowing the answer.

"Out. She went to the movies with her...friend, remember?"

Nathan settled back on the sofa. "Ah, that's right. She went to the movies with Sara." He grinned at Emma. "Did you get to meet the lovely Sara?"

Emma glanced away. "No. I was unpacking when the doorbell rang."

Nathan nodded, wondering just how far Emma was willing to go to protect Leigh. "Too bad. Sara's very nice. I'm sure you'll like her. So why didn't you go to the movies with them?"

"I had some reading to catch up on."

"I see. So, it wasn't the fact that you'd be in the way on Leigh's wild date that kept you home?"

Emma met his gaze dead on. "You knew?"

"Even before I left, I suspected her friend was going to be someone with a five-o'clock shadow and an Adam's apple who was named Mike or Keith or Horatio."

A bubble of laughter escaped Emma. "Horatio? Hardly."

"Yeah. I know." He watched her for a second, then

said, "His name's Jared. He's a rodeo rider. And I could skin Leigh alive for going out with him."

Emma set the stack of papers she'd been reading on the coffee table in front of her, then asked, "Pardon me for interfering, but why do you care? Leigh's twenty-one. She's more than old enough to make her own decisions. You should let her choose her own friends."

Nathan couldn't help smiling at Emma's statement. "In theory, you have a point, and normally, I'd agree with you. Someone her age doesn't need to be supervised. Or at least, they shouldn't need to be supervised. But in reality, this is Leigh we are discussing. She causes more problems than a rattlesnake at a rodeo."

That made her laugh. "I am seeing that side of her now," she admitted.

"Plus, this is Honey, Texas. Folks around here watch out for their family members."

His comment earned him a doubting look from Emma. "I think people around the world watch out for their family members. It's not unique to Honey, Texas."

He shrugged. "True. But here in Honey, if I don't show an interest in my sister's life, I will hear about it from half the population. The folks around here like to meddle."

"So I've heard," Emma admitted with a chuckle.

"That's a small town for you. Were you born in Texas?" he asked, enjoying this conversation more than he'd expected.

Emma shook her head. "No. I've only been in Texas for five years. Before that, my mother and I moved fairly often."

That explained a lot. "And if I had to guess, I'd say you're an only child."

"Right." She leaned forward, her expression intense. "None of that matters. What the town thinks doesn't matter. No offense, but you shouldn't meddle in your sister's life. You may think you know what she should do, but it's her life and her choices."

There were very few things Nathan enjoyed more than a good argument with a worthy opponent. Emma was definitely a worthy opponent.

"Leigh means the world to me. I don't want to see her hurt," he said simply.

"You need to trust her instincts."

He had to laugh at that one. "Really? Would those be the instincts that convinced her dying her hair bright green in high school was a terrific idea? Or the instincts that told her taking up motocross racing would be a great way to meet guys but failed to mention that she could end up dead? Or the instincts that caused her to ignore the teacher's directives in chemistry class, so she proceeded to blow up the classroom. Sorry, Emma, but Leigh's got questionable instincts."

"Wow, I didn't know she blew up a classroom. I hope no one was hurt."

When he shook his head, she smiled. "Thank goodness. Sorry. I know I shouldn't interfere, but I have to wonder if you and your brothers hover over each other as much as you hover over Leigh."

"That's okay. It's good to hear your thoughts." He returned her smile. "My brothers and I do watch out for each other, but you're right. We probably hover more over Leigh."

"Because she's female," Emma suggested.

"No. Because she's young and fairly wild," he countered. "Leigh is like her own personal tornado. She goes through life leaving a path of destruction behind her. Look at your life. She would have really messed it up if I hadn't helped."

He could tell she was uncertain what to say, but he knew she realized he was right. Maybe he was a little sexist when it came to his only sister, but he also was a realist.

Deciding to lighten the mood, he smiled. "At least she keeps life interesting—sort of like a nest of rattlesnakes."

Emma laughed and nodded. "True."

For a second, they simply looked at each other, quiet peace settling over them. Then, before he knew it, the atmosphere in the room seemed to suddenly shift. Awareness sparked, then danced between them.

Not a good thing.

Since this little chat was becoming way too cozy, he looked away. "It's early yet. Want to take a walk? I can show you the sights of Honey."

"Honey has sights?"

He laughed. "Of course, it has sights. Lots of them. How very big-city of you to think otherwise. You shouldn't miss this opportunity."

Emma glanced at the papers on the coffee table. "As tempting as the idea of a walk sounds, I really should work."

Nathan decided to up his offer. "You sure I can't lure you away for just a while? Honey is world-renowned for its fabulous ice cream. We could stop by the ice cream parlor and get a double scoop."

"Let me get this straight; you live in a small town that has a world-famous ice cream parlor? Is this a Norman Rockwell picture or what?"

Nathan stood and extended his hand. "Why don't you come with me and find out?"

For a heartbeat, Emma looked up at him. Then with a small sigh, she took his hand and stood. "All I want to know is if this ice cream parlor is world-renowned, why haven't I even heard of it?"

Nathan reluctantly let go of her hand, then waited for Emma to precede him out of the house. "I guess you've been hanging out in the wrong part of the world," he teased.

Emma laughed, the sound carefree and light. Nathan couldn't help smiling, enjoying himself for the first time in a long while. After they walked down the driveway, he headed them toward the center of town.

"I know you think you've distracted me, but you haven't. Before we left the house, we were discussing Leigh."

Nathan tipped his head and looked at her. "We were?"

"Yes, we were. I was pointing out that you should let her make her own decisions." Emma's soft voice settled over him like a warm mist. "And let her clean up her own messes."

For the briefest of moments, Nathan allowed himself the luxury of simply looking at Emma. Then he said, "I don't think I could butt out of her life if I wanted to. Worrying about her is coded in my DNA."

"Hi, Mr. Barrett."

Nathan stopped and turned. The McCluskey twins were weeding in their garden. He smiled at the teen girls, the daughters of one of his lead programmers. "Hi, Debbie. Hi, Carrie. How are you ladies today?"

The girls giggled and blushed, although for the life of him, he didn't know why.

"We're excellent," said Debbie. "Really excellent." She looked at Emma and shyly said, "Hi."

Nathan quickly introduced Emma to the girls, explaining that Emma was going to work for Barrett Software.

"I'm going to work at Barrett Software after I get through college," Carrie said, dusting her hands off on her red shorts and leaving black marks. "I'm going to be a programmer like Dad."

"Me, too." Debbie smiled at him. "I can't wait until I can work there."

"It's great you two have your future mapped out," Emma said. "When I was your age, I wanted to cure world hunger or be a rock star."

"That's because you didn't have Barrett Software as your third choice," Nathan teased.

"We've got it all planned," Carrie said. "It's going to be excellent."

And after a couple of minutes catching up, Nathan wished the girls a good evening, and he and Emma headed on toward town.

"You have two not-so-secret admirers there," Emma said after they'd walked half a block.

Nathan glanced at her. "They're a couple of great kids. That's all."

Emma smiled. "I don't think so. I think they think you're *excellent*."

Rather than answering, he put his hand on her arm, stopping her. "Hold on a second. You're going to step on Rufus if you're not careful."

"Rufus?"

Nathan nodded at the hound dog sprawled across the sidewalk up ahead. "Rufus."

Emma let out a small gasp. "That's a dog?" She edged slowly closer, and as usual, Rufus didn't bother to move. "I caught it out of the corner of my eye, and I thought it was some kind of dog-shaped fungus growing on the sidewalk."

By now they were almost directly in front of the dog. When Emma went to bend toward the mutt, Nathan stopped her again.

"Rufus doesn't like to be bothered. Just step over him."

Emma blinked. "Does he bite?"

"No, he's just a gentleman who prefers his own company," Nathan explained, laughing at the incredulous expression on her face. He carefully stepped over Rufus, then turned and helped Emma across.

"Is he sick? Shouldn't his owner take him to the vet?"

"Rufus is as healthy as a horse. He's simply mellow and likes to snooze. The vet says it's his personality. Besides, he livens up when a car approaches."

"He chases cars?"

"No, not chases. But he barks at them," Nathan said. "Sometimes. When the mood strikes him."

"But he could run out into the road and get hit. This is very dangerous."

Nathan leaned down and showed her the leash on Rufus' collar. "If he tried, he'd be stopped. Several of us helped install the leash to make sure nothing bad happened to him. He's only outside a little while each day, and when he is, he's able to wander around the yard. He never does, though. He just flops on the sidewalk and snoozes. We all know when he's sleeping to step over him."

Emma shook her head. "Strange."

"That's Honey for you. We like our little idiosyncrasies." Nathan headed them down Main Street. "So, tell me, how did you meet Leigh? No offense, but you don't seem to have a lot in common."

"Why not? Leigh's nice, and fun, and—"

"Crazy, and devious, and irresponsible at times." When Emma laughed, Nathan found himself looking at her lips and couldn't help wondering if they felt as soft as they appeared.

With effort, he pulled his gaze away from her lips and studied her face. "So, how'd you meet?"

"We both used to hang out in the library, and after a while, we started talking. Eventually we became friends."

That didn't sound like his sister at all. "The library? Leigh hung out in the library?"

"Yes, she was there quite a lot. I think you underestimate her. She takes her studies very seriously."

Although Leigh was getting decent grades in college, Nathan knew for a fact those grades came without a lot of time devoted to studying. She was a fast learner, and college came easily to her. An unsettled feeling crawled over him like a bug. Something didn't add up.

"Was she at the library at a certain time of day?" he asked.

Emma frowned. "Why?"

"I'd be willing to bet there was a guy who worked there at the times that Leigh was around."

Emma laughed softly. "You really are suspicious of her, aren't you?"

"I'm not suspicious. I'm a realist."

Apparently not buying his explanation, Emma's frown deepened. "Are you suspicious of everyone or just Leigh?"

Oh, now this was getting fun. "Just Leigh. I trust most people."

They were outside Monroe's Drug Store. Out of habit and training, Nathan held the door for a local man, George Brown, who was coming out carrying several large bags.

"Hey there, Nathan," George said, shifting his packages and shaking Nathan's hand. Leaning close, he said, "I should tell you, I saw Leigh going into the movies with Jared Kendrick earlier tonight. You know 'bout that?"

Nathan nodded. "I know. How are you?"

George narrowed his gaze and for a second looked as if he was going to say more, but then he noticed Emma. "Well, hello there. I don't think we've met."

Nathan quickly introduced them, and George shook Emma's hand. "You're going to like working at Barrett Software. Great place." He slapped Nathan on the back. "The boy here has done good by this town. But we always knew he would. After he took the football team to State, we knew Honey could count on him."

"We didn't win," Nathan felt compelled to point out.

"But you gave it your all, Nathan. That's what counts."

After helping George load his bags into his car, Nathan waved goodbye and started walking again. It took him a couple of seconds to realize Emma wasn't walking with him.

"Everything okay?" he asked.

She slowly approached him, humor lurking in her eyes. "Tell me, does everyone in this town think you're the best thing since microwave popcorn, or are we just running into the zealots?"

3

"I have friends in Honey." Nathan chuckled. "That's why I opened my business here."

"Friends? More like fans." She nodded toward the restored courthouse building that now housed Barrett Software. "You should be proud of what you've accomplished. It looks like your company keeps this town going."

Nathan idly kicked a stone on the sidewalk, not really comfortable with the praise. "I've helped Honey, sure, but this town was a great place long before I opened Barrett Software."

She smiled at him, a pretty smile that made her eyes sparkle. "If you say so," she teased. "But I can hardly wait to see who else we meet on our little stroll. I'm feeling pretty popular since I'm going for ice cream with the captain of the football team."

"That was a long time ago," he pointed out. Wanting to talk about anything other than himself, he turned the tables. "You know way too much about me. Tell me about yourself instead."

For a second, she hesitated. Then she said, "Fine. We'll change the subject. We'll no longer discuss your glory days." She tipped her head and looked downright adorable. "Let's see. About me. Well, like I said, I'm working on my doctorate in English. End of story."

Nathan chuckled. "Ah. So, you didn't start out as a baby, then grow up to be a teenager, and finally turn into a woman? You popped out of the womb a full-fledged Ph.D. candidate?"

Her smile was sassy. "Wouldn't that have been a time saver? But you're right. I started out the boring, usual way."

When she didn't expand on her answer, he teased, "You're a chatty thing, aren't you? You keep on with these stories, and you'll burn my ears off."

"Oh, fine, but if we're playing twenty questions here, you go first. Tell me about you. I already know you're adored in the town where you grew up and that you led the football team to State, which makes you a real hero around here. Tell me the rest."

Nathan started them walking toward the ice cream store again. "The abridged version is I'm thirty-three with a master's in computer science from UT. I've never been married. My favorite food is lobster, but don't tell anyone around here because it should be steak since this is Texas. My favorite movie is *Die Hard*." At Emma's smug look, he admitted, "I know. What a male stereo-type, but I like it. My favorite book is—"

Emma held up one hand. "Let me guess, *Catcher in the Rye*."

"And yours is probably *Jane Eyre*."

"*To Kill a Mockingbird*."

"Ah. I stand corrected. And your favorite movie is probably *Pretty Woman*."

She wrinkled her nose and ran one hand through her hair. "No."

"*Sleepless in Seattle?*"

"No. It's—"

"Let me guess." Determined to figure this out, Nathan scanned his brain for all the romantic movies he knew. Landing on one more, he asked, "*While You Were Sleeping?*"

She beamed. "Yes. Were you going to guess every chick flick you could think of until you got it right?"

He chuckled. He really liked talking to Emma. She was smart and interesting. "Of course. There was a principle at stake."

"What principle would that be?"

"The principle that says I'm never wrong," he told her.

She laughed again, and Nathan felt the simmering attraction between them heat up a couple more degrees.

"Okay, what else do you want to know?" she asked.

He thought for a moment, then asked, "Tell me about your first crush."

She seemed surprised, but she didn't hesitate. "Donald Freed, when I was ten. I thought he was wonderful."

"Did you ever tell him?"

"No. And it was a good thing since I'd gotten over

the crush by the time I was ten and a quarter. How about you? Who was your first crush on?"

"Sally Jean Myerson, fourth grade." He couldn't start a smile from crossing his face at the memory.

"Did you ever confess your love?"

"Nah, she liked another boy in class, and I didn't want to ruin their budding relationship."

"How noble."

Honesty forced him to admit, "Well, her boyfriend was the size of two semis. He would have beat the stuffing out of me, so I decided to find someone else to like."

"Noble and wise. Good combination."

"So, this Donald Freed, was he good-looking?" Nathan asked.

"He was cute, but what I really liked was that he was predictable. Not into a lot of drama. I found that appealing. At least for one quarter of a year."

"I take it you like quiet, boring men, then?"

Again, she ran one hand through her hair, and Nathan's gaze followed the gesture. He really did like the shade of her hair. The fading sun seemed to make it gleam.

"What can I tell you? I've got low standards," Emma said.

"I'm pretty boring," Nathan found himself saying, then immediately wished he hadn't. He shouldn't be flirting with this woman. She was only in town for the summer. Plus, she was going to work for him.

And most importantly, whether she knew it or not, she was being used by Leigh as bait. He knew it just like he knew the sun would rise in the east tomorrow—Leigh was up to something.

Fortunately, Emma didn't seem to read anything into his comment. She shook her head and said, "I seriously doubt you're boring, so I'm afraid it won't work."

He snapped his fingers, still keeping the tone light and teasing. "Dang it. Okay, so tell me about your family."

"Well, my mom raised me."

"By herself?"

Emma nodded. "Yes. She was a lot of fun. Big on adventures. She loved to pack up and move someplace new at a moment's notice just to see what life was like in a different sort of place. One day we'd live in the mountains, then we'd go live by the ocean for a few months. It was never boring around my mom." A soft smile lit her face. "She passed away a little over two years ago. I really miss her."

"She sounds like a great lady. What about your father?"

"He teaches at Wyneheart College, just west of Boston. I didn't get to spend a lot of time with him when I was growing up, but he always sent money and called frequently."

"He's the only family you have left?"

"Yes." She stopped to look in one of the store windows, then added, "But I'm finally going to get to spend time with him. He's arranged an adjunct teaching position for me at the college after I get my doctorate."

Happiness radiated off her. Nathan could tell how much this meant to her.

"Congratulations on the job and on getting to

connect with your dad," he said. "I've heard of Wyne-heart. It's a good college."

Emma nodded. "It's wonderful. And I'll get to focus on American Literature, which is my specialty." After a slight pause, she added, "I haven't told a soul this. Not even Leigh. But I'm really looking forward to living in the town of Wyneheart. It's wonderful. Small, but seeped in history. Very cozy."

Nathan completely understood the appeal. "Kind of like Honey."

Emma blinked and frowned at him. Slowly she looked around Main Street, then finally said, "Um. I guess."

He couldn't help laughing at her dumbfounded expression. "Okay. I know this may not look like Wyneheart, which was probably built by the Pilgrims, but Honey has a lot of history. True Wild West history."

Her expression was openly dubious, but she still asked, "Such as?"

"Such as rumor has it that Wyatt Earp once ate at the local diner."

"Is that true?"

"Everyone says it is, and Wyatt's not around to argue, so we accept it as fact."

She laughed, which made him smile. He loved the sound of her laughter.

"What else?" she asked.

He thought for a second. "Bonnie and Clyde drove through town one time."

"Really?"

He had to bite back a smile. "Well, the car was

moving very fast, but everyone was almost positive it was them."

She laughed. "Seems like the history of this town is a little shaky."

"Okay, here's a certifiable fact. For five years in the 1880s, Honey housed more establishments for the entertainment of gentlemen than any other city in Texas, including the big cities."

It took only a fraction of a second for her to get his meaning. Then she laughed again. "You're kidding me, right?"

He solemnly shook his head. "Nope. It's true. We didn't just get the name 'honey' because of the number of bees around here."

"Honey had that many bordellos?"

"Yes, ma'am. It was called Heaven on Earth. But then settlers moved in and chased off the no-goods."

She rolled her eyes. "What a place."

"It suits me."

"So, it seems. Tell me about Barrett Software."

Now that was his favorite subject. "We're doing well. Better than I'd hoped and growing each year. That accounting program I told you about should really put us on the map. That is, if we can get the bugs out in time to unveil it at the BizExpo, the Dallas computer show later this summer."

"The program is that good?"

"Got all the bells and whistles. It's easy to use, works on all platforms, and is voice-controlled."

"That's what I'll be helping with?"

"Yes. That's what everyone is working on. Mostly though, you'll be handling me."

She tipped her head. "Want to try that again?"

He chuckled, although just the thought of her touching him was enough to get his blood pressure climbing.

"Since you'll be my assistant, you'll have to keep my schedule straight," he explained, trying to keep his wayward mind on track. "It gets crazy sometimes. Devi, my assistant who's out on maternity leave, says it's a spider's web. Just when you get it straight and looking nice, you realize there's a big old spider sitting in the middle that you overlooked."

She laughed again. "Don't worry. I'm very organized. I'll keep the spider away from you."

They had reached Honey Ice Cream Parlor, so Nathan didn't ask for clarification on the last part of her statement. Instead, he held the door open for her. As Emma passed, her sweet scent taunted him again.

"Well, if it isn't Nathan Barrett," Caitlin Estes, owner of the shop, said when she saw him. "It's about time you stopped by. You're harder to find than a mouse at a cat wedding."

"Hi, Caitlin." He nodded toward Emma. "This is Emma Montgomery. She's a friend of Leigh's who's going to work at Barrett Software for the summer."

The look Caitlin gave Emma wasn't exactly cold, but Nathan wasn't obtuse enough to think the two women would become friends. Not that he was surprised. Caitlin had made it clear since she'd been head cheerleader in high school that she wanted to be a lot more than merely an acquaintance of his. It wasn't a sentiment he reciprocated.

"It's nice to meet you," Emma said. Then she must

have figured the ice cream was warmer than Caitlin because she moved away and studied the flavors on display in the cases.

"Since you almost never come to see me, I'm going to have to find a way to visit you at your office," Caitlin said, flashing him a flirty smile.

Nathan was very careful to keep his expression neutral. He knew how easily looks could be misinterpreted. "I appreciate the idea, Caitlin, but we're really busy right now."

Caitlin ran one finger under the thin strap of her T-shirt and winked. Now that was about as subtle as a smack to the head. "Not too busy for a little fun, I hope. I think we should spend some time together."

He didn't agree, but he also didn't want to hurt her feelings. "Normally I like having friends stop by the office, but I doubt if I'd have time to see you. Thanks anyway."

Caitlin pouted. "I'm not giving up that easily, Nathan Barrett. I guess I'll have to get creative."

Her down mood didn't last long, because before she'd formed a really impressive pout, she brightened and asked, "Hey, did you hear that Leigh's out with Jared Kendrick? Did you know about that?"

"Yes, I know." Glancing toward Emma, he found her watching him closely. Before he could say anything else to Caitlin, a crowd of young boys came in and snagged her attention. Relieved, Nathan moved over to join Emma. She stood looking into one of the large display cases that contained a dazzling array of ice creams.

"Have you decided?" he asked.

She glanced up at him. "I'd like a single scoop of vanilla."

He laughed and nodded toward the ice cream case. "That's it? All these amazing choices and you want vanilla?"

Emma shrugged. "Some of us know a good thing when we find it, and once our decision is made, we stick to it. I'm a vanilla purist."

She waved her hand at the multitude of flavors. "Let me guess. You want something wild like—" She glanced in the ice cream case again and said, "Loopy, Luscious Lemon? Or maybe Crazy, Cookey Coconut?"

Nathan smiled. "Not exactly."

Behind him, he heard Caitlin laugh. "Are you kidding? This guy is loyal to the end. It's vanilla all the way for him."

Nathan leaned against the display case and smiled at Emma. "I guess that makes two of us who stick with a good thing once we find it."

❧

"THE FAX WORKS BETTER IF YOU GIVE IT A GOOD whack," Leigh said from the doorway to Emma's office the next morning. "Here, let me show you."

Emma had been carefully reading the instruction manual, but now she looked at Leigh and moved the fax out of the younger woman's reach. "Don't you dare hit it."

Leigh stopped midstride and grinned. "You're just like Nathan—sentimental. It's a machine, not a person.

He should have gotten rid of that piece of junk years ago, but he keeps getting it fixed."

Emma shifted the fax even farther from Leigh's grasp, then leaned back in her chair. "I'm positive the fax can be fixed. It just sticks a little."

With a laugh, Leigh dropped into the chair facing Emma's desk. "I can't believe you're defending a fax machine." She glanced around the office. "Any other equipment you've grown attached to already?"

Emma relaxed for the first time this morning. She was really glad Leigh had dropped by. Her new job made her tense. Everyone at Barrett Software seemed tense. If the accounting program, Simplify, wasn't error-free by the Dallas computer show, Barrett Software would miss a wonderful opportunity to introduce the product to the public. Building up a market would be so much more difficult without the added exposure.

For her part, Emma wanted to do well, and so far this morning, she'd eaten four antacids. Leigh was exactly what she needed to calm down.

"I'm rather fond of the computer and the printer, now that you ask," Emma said.

Leigh's expression turned downright mischievous. "How about my hunky brother? Gotten attached to him yet?"

Okay, so much for calming down. Just the mention of Nathan was enough to get her pulse racing. "He's very nice."

"Nice? So that's why you went with him for ice cream last night? Because he's nice?"

Emma wasn't the least surprised that Leigh knew about their walk through town. Emma figured that she'd met most of the population of Honey during the stroll home. People had seemed to pop out from every direction, and Nathan had been charming to everyone they'd met. By the end of the evening, Emma had to admit she'd been more than a little charmed herself. She wanted to believe it was the night and the companionship of an attractive man that had made her reluctant to see the evening end, but that was bunk.

The reason she'd hated for last night to end was that she'd had a terrific time with Nathan Barrett. But she'd rather dye her hair purple with pink stripes than admit that to Leigh.

So to be on the safe side, all Emma was willing to admit was, "Nathan was very nice to take me for ice cream. He thought I might be bored."

Leigh laughed. "Yeah, good old Nathan. He's a real sport to entertain a lonely lady."

"I appreciated it. I enjoyed finding out about Honey." Deciding it was past time to turn this conversation around, Emma said, "I heard you had a fun date last night."

Rather than looking contrite, Leigh's smile only grew. "That I did, as everyone in Honey knows. Nothing like having your every move telegraphed around town."

"A lot of people did seem to know about your date."

Leigh shrugged. "Typical Honey. Information capital of the world. If you sneeze, people two miles away say bless you."

Yesterday, Emma would have thought Leigh was exaggerating, but after the walk last night, she knew better. "I'll keep that in mind."

Leigh glanced around the office. "So other than the fax machine, are you getting settled in? I feel terrible for not getting up early this morning and coming into the office with you. Sorry I overslept."

"Leigh, Honey only has four major streets. It wasn't like negotiating New York City."

"Well, there is that tricky bit on Pine Street where Rufus will bark frantically at your car if you're not quick."

Emma had to laugh at that one. "I met Rufus last night. All he did when I drove by this morning was woof once at me. He didn't bark frantically at my car."

Leigh tapped her temple. "In his head he did. Rufus is more cerebral than physical, but we don't like to tell him that. We all pretend he scares us. Makes him feel he's important around here."

Emma shook her head. "This place is insane."

"That's called charm," Nathan said.

Emma glanced up to find him standing in the doorway to her office. He smiled at her then at his sister. "Hello, ladies."

Nathan had a twinkle in his eyes when he looked at Emma. He was so amazingly handsome in his dark-blue suit, her breath caught in her throat. She smiled when she noticed he wore cowboy boots with his suit.

"Nice boots," she said.

He grinned. A lopsided grin that was downright sexy. "This is Texas after all."

For several long seconds, he held Emma's gaze. With effort, she pulled her attention away and cleared her throat. "Your ten o'clock appointment is here. Caitlin Estes is in your office."

Nathan frowned. "Caitlin's here. Why?"

"She said she's from the Honey Ladies' Society." A feeling of dread settled in Emma's stomach. His expression made it pretty clear he hadn't been expecting Caitlin. "Is something wrong?"

Leigh made a snorting noise. "Caitlin wants to be the head of Nathan's fan club."

Emma looked at her friend. "What?"

"Don't worry about it," Nathan told her. Then he turned to his sister. "Speaking of people who shouldn't be here, Leigh, what brings you here?"

"I stopped by to see Emma." Leigh looked at Emma, then back at her brother. "Wanted to make certain that ice cream she had last night settled okay."

"Sure you didn't stop by to talk about the movie you saw last night?"

Leigh laughed. "As if. I'm not telling you about my personal life, Nathan, so forget it."

"Just as well. My heart probably couldn't stand the details." He looked at Emma and asked, "Are you getting settled?"

"Yes, thanks." And so far, with the exception of Caitlin, everything else had gone fine. A young woman from personnel had gotten her started, and the morning had flown by. With the exception of the temperamental fax machine, she'd had no problem figuring out the equipment. She'd even taken some time to organize a few of Nathan's files. Plus, she'd printed out his schedule. Despite her jittery nerves, everything was happening like clockwork. "No problems."

"Good." His gaze met hers again, and sure enough, her heart did a little thumpity-thump. What was it about this man that got to her so? She wasn't the type to let hormones cloud her judgment, but boy did they ever when he was around.

Emma scrambled to think of something to say to him, anything at all, but she simply couldn't get her mind in gear.

Finally, he solved her problem by saying, "If you have any questions, just let me know."

"I have a question," Leigh said. "Why haven't you tossed this old fax into the garbage? It's junk, Nathan. You're too sentimental."

Nathan glanced at the machine in question, then looked at Emma. "You can swap it with the one in my office if it's giving you too many problems."

"No, I'm sure I'll be able to figure it out," she said.

Nathan glanced at the closed door to his office, then returned his attention to Emma. "So Caitlin, huh?"

Emma glanced at his schedule. " Yes. She said she was from the Honey Ladies' Society."

"I can't believe Caitlin did this." Nathan frowned. "She's not with the—" He stopped when the elevator door opened, and a middle-aged woman exited. "Emma, this is Amanda Newman. She heads up the Honey Ladies' Society."

Amanda walked forward, her gaze moving from Emma to Leigh to Nathan. "Am I late?"

Leigh laughed. "From what I can tell, Amanda, you're right on time. Seems Caitlin pretended to be from the Ladies' Society and is waiting in Nathan's office."

Amanda frowned. "I wish they'd stop doing this."

Truly baffled, Emma had to ask, "Doing what?"

Nathan glanced at his closed door. "It's kind of a joke around town. Some of the single ladies occasionally try to...trick their way into seeing me. I'm busy and like to keep personal callers off my calendar, unless it's for charity. Which is why Amanda is here."

Emma studied the closed door. What had she done? "So Ms. Estes isn't with the Ladies' Society?"

Laughter sputtered from Leigh. "Not even close. Caitlin just wanted to get in to see Nathan and snagged this opportunity. Emma, don't feel badly. Lots of the local ladies do this kind of thing to him all the time. They're trying to find ways to get his attention. They do things like delivering pies here or sending him truck-loads of flowers." She slapped Nathan on the back. "My brother is one hot property."

Amanda sighed. "I shouldn't have mentioned that I was coming to see Nathan to so many people. I'll talk to Caitlin."

Before she could move, Leigh held up one hand. "No way, Mrs. Newman. Caitlin went to a lot of trouble. Let's not spoil it."

A feeling of dread settled low in Emma's stomach. She felt terrible that she'd let this woman into Nathan's office. And since she'd caused the problem, she'd also be the one to solve it.

"I'll ask her to leave since she misled me." Emma took a step forward, but Leigh skirted around her.

"I want to see what Caitlin's cooked up." Practically skipping, Leigh threw open the door.

Loud, pulsating music immediately started. Leigh and Nathan were the first ones inside the office.

Emma heard Leigh's laughter and what sounded like

a groan from Nathan. When she and Amanda Newman reached the doorway, they both froze.

For her own part, all Emma could do was stare. Caitlin Estes was dressed in what appeared to be a cheerleader's uniform. She was performing a variety of routines for Nathan, and Emma would give her this— Caitlin Estes was one limber lady. She did flips. She did tumbles. She jumped and cheered and hooted.

"I guess the ladies in town have tried about everything now," Amanda murmured when Caitlin did an impressive handstand right in front of Nathan, her little skirt flipping up to display a big red heart tattooed on her left thigh.

Finally, with a hop, Caitlin stood and grinned at Nathan. "Let me know if you want to see my other tattoos," she said with a wink. Then as calmly as could be, Caitlin put her coat back on, shut off the music on her phone, and left the office, wagging her fingers in a wave to the rest of the group as she went by.

"Well, that was different," Amanda said after Caitlin got in the elevator.

"I can't believe she did that," Nathan observed dryly, walking over to his desk.

Emma looked at him, trying to gauge his reaction to what had just happened. Thankfully he didn't seem angry. He also didn't appear upset or flustered, and a small part of Emma was thrilled to see he didn't seem the least bit intrigued by what had happened. Mostly he seemed amused.

Still, she felt terrible. Here she'd promised to be the perfect assistant, and then she'd gone and let that woman in. She should have questioned Caitlin more carefully, but she'd assumed the young woman was being honest.

That would teach her to make assumptions. She'd let the small-town, laid-back atmosphere of Honey fool her, and so far, her first day on the job was off to a dismal start.

"Could have been worse," Leigh pointed out. "At least Caitlin was wearing panties."

❦

NATHAN PULLED INTO HIS DRIVEWAY, PUT HIS CAR IN Park, and let out a long sigh. Home. Finally. After what had to be one of the longest days of his life. Simplify had more bugs than an ant farm. He'd spent most of his day helping with the testing and making suggestions on fixes.

He'd expected problems because a program as complicated as this one always had bugs. But BizExpo was only a six weeks away, and Barrett Software needed to make a big splash there if the company was going to keep supporting most of the town of Honey.

Normally he considered himself a fairly lucky guy, but not today. Today he figured he stood a pretty good chance of a house dropping on him, and it was with a great deal of caution that he opened his car door and climbed out. For one second, he held his breath, waiting for another catastrophe to bonk him on the head.

Thankfully, though, nothing happened.

Until he heard the thumping noise coming from over on the sports court. Before he could consider the wisdom of investigating, he glanced that way. Emma was playing basketball on the court, and from the way she was pushing herself, she was working off the tension of her day.

For a heartbeat, he simply watched her, enjoying the enticing sight. And Emma Montgomery was indeed a sight, with her long legs and curvy body.

Although he didn't make a sound, she must have sensed him watching her because she turned and looked at him.

"Hi," she said, breathing fast.

"Hi." Nathan wandered over to the court and set his briefcase down on the bench. "You've been playing hard."

She dribbled the ball a few times. "Want to take your best shot?"

Although there was nothing sexual about her comment, his gaze snagged hers. He knew he should say no and head on inside the house, but his mind couldn't seem to get his body to respond.

"Sure," he said, shrugging out of his jacket and tossing it on top of his briefcase. She handed him the ball. He sized up his shot, then watched with satisfaction as the ball whooshed through the hoop.

"Nice shot," she said, picking up the ball.

"That's the first thing that's gone right today," he admitted.

Emma stopped a couple of feet from him, and her smile faded. "I am so sorry about what happened with Caitlin. I had no idea she intended on doing...what she did. She was wearing a nice coat when she arrived."

Nathan laughed. "Don't worry about that. Caitlin

and her friends are always doing stuff to me. They've been doing it for years."

Emma slowly shook her head. "How can that not bother you? And to think, I let her into your office. I'll be much more careful in the future."

He admired Emma's dedication to a job she'd just started. The woman was a hard worker and realized how important this program was to Barrett Software. Knowing a type-A personality like Emma was going to let the Caitlin incident gnaw at her, Nathan decided a distraction was in order.

He snagged the basketball out of her arms and started to dribble it.

"Let's forget about work. First one to twenty points wins." Then before Emma could say a word, he went by her and easily sunk the ball. "Two points for me."

"Hey, that's not fair. I didn't even agree to play."

Nathan grinned. "Too late. I'm winning. What are you going to do about it?"

Emma opened her mouth, and for a second, he thought she was going to refuse to play. But then abruptly, she grinned right back at him. "You're on."

Although he wasn't dressed for a game of basketball, he managed to keep up with Emma. But just barely. The woman was good. Very good. By the time they were tied at eighteen points each, Nathan was sweating and breathing hard.

"This is it," Emma said, easily moving the ball from hand to hand. "Hold on, Nathan Barrett, I'm going to wipe the court with you."

He laughed. "In your dreams."

Emma started dribbling down the court, then

veered left, but he moved with her. She tried to recover and go right, but he blocked her again. Finally, she turned and went to scoot past him, but he was too quick for her. He knocked the ball out of her hands, and when he lunged for it, he ended up bumping into Emma.

"Whoa." He wrapped his arms around her waist and barely kept her from falling over. At first she teetered, and he almost lost his footing as well. But finally, they managed to steady themselves.

"Well, that was graceful," Emma said with a laugh. She blew out a breath and ruffled her bangs.

"Want to call it a draw before we kill ourselves?"

She smiled. "Probably a smart idea."

For a second, he returned her smile. Then he realized he still had his arms around her waist. Her hands were on his shoulders. And her warm, soft body was pressed against him. Without meaning to, he glanced at her full lips.

Let her go, you idiot.

His hands didn't move, and neither did hers. He met her gaze. He could see the same fire of attraction in her eyes that he felt burning inside of him. "I should—"

"We can't—"

He nodded. "Right. I know."

She nodded. "Absolutely. Not smart."

He looked at her again. Her hands still hadn't moved. Neither had his. He could feel his heart thumping wildly in his chest. He needed to be smart. He needed to exercise willpower.

Emma's gaze dropped to his lips. Then slowly, she leaned toward him.

Ah, hell. He needed to get this situation under control before something happened that they'd both regret.

Her lips brushed his.

And his good intentions dried up and blew away.

4

Emma hadn't really meant to kiss Nathan. Sure, she'd wanted to—very much so. But she hadn't meant to actually do it. Kissing him wasn't a bright thing to do. Kissing him could lead to all sorts of problems.

But now that she was actually wrapped in his arms and kissing him for all she was worth, she had to admit it was pretty darn terrific. Nathan Barrett kissed like he did everything else—well. Very, very well.

As he deepened the kiss, tingles danced over her sensitized skin. Yep, the man could kiss. Oh, boy and how. He kissed so well that she pushed aside all the annoying reasons why she shouldn't be doing this and simply enjoyed herself. Nathan, too, seemed to be caught up in the kiss.

Emma had no idea how long they stood on the basketball court kissing, but it was a long, long time. Even so, when Nathan finally broke the kiss, she couldn't help feeling disappointed.

Her disappointment only increased when he slowly removed his arms from around her and took a step back. Now that they were no longer touching, the air between them crackled with a combination of lust and regret.

Nathan cleared his throat. "I didn't mean to do that. It was completely unfair, and I hope you know I didn't mean to take advantage of you."

His comment was completely expected, and the last thing Emma wanted to hear. But he was right. Now was the time to backpedal like crazy away from what had happened.

"What do you mean? Why was it unfair?" She really was baffled. She felt many things after that kiss, but she sure didn't feel like he'd taken advantage of her.

"You work for me, and you live here. It was reprehensible of me to kiss you."

Emma couldn't help it. She smiled. "I understand why you feel that way, but technically, you didn't kiss me. I was the one who started this, and in no way did you take advantage of me." She scuffed the toe of her sneaker on the ground. "Still. I can't imagine why I did that."

Oh, great. She sounded like an idiot. Plus, she was a liar. She knew exactly why she'd kissed him—the man was hotter than an August afternoon in Texas.

But Nathan didn't question her explanation. Instead, he acted like the perfect gentleman he always seemed to be. His expression was concerned. "That kiss was more my fault than yours, Emma."

The intellectual side of her forced her to ask, "No offense, but how do you figure that? I was the one who kissed you first. How does that make it your fault?"

"I could have stopped you."

"Hardly."

"Of course, I could have."

She was skeptical. "I think you'll need to come up with a better explanation. I still don't see how it's your fault."

He opened his mouth, then promptly shut it. Emma couldn't help smiling as she watched him struggle for an answer—one he never did end up finding.

"See, I'm right," she said with a laugh when he still hadn't come up with a reason after a few seconds. "It is my fault, not yours. Please stop worrying about this. I didn't feel pressured, and it had nothing to do with my job or my living arrangement. The kiss wasn't your fault."

He flashed a rueful grin, and Emma was glad the atmosphere between them lightened.

"I haven't given up yet," he said. "I only need a couple more minutes, and I'll think of a reason why I'm to blame."

She shook her head. "Nope. Time's up. You have to admit it was my fault."

Her teasing accomplished what she'd hoped it would. They were no longer awkward and uncomfortable with each other. Instead, they were joking and laughing about the kiss. For her part, Emma had never felt less like laughing in her life. That kiss had shaken her clear to her toes.

But Nathan had been right. The kiss never should have happened, and since she had to work with this man, self-preservation demanded they put what had happened behind them. Way far behind them.

Nathan raised one eyebrow. "Are you always so opinionated?"

She nodded. "Absolutely. And it's not that I'm opinionated. It's that I'm always right."

He laughed and scooped the ball up off the ground. "Why don't we agree that regardless of who started the whole kissing thing, we shouldn't have done it? We do have to work together."

"Exactly."

He dribbled the basketball a couple of times, then added, "And I don't think either one of us is looking to start something."

"True. I'm only here for the summer." She shifted her weight from one foot to the other and tried to ignore the nervous bubbling in her stomach. This was becoming awkward again. Now seemed like a wonderful time to escape. "I think I'll go shower," she said, grabbing the first excuse that popped into her mind.

Nathan dribbled the basketball. "Okay. I think I'll stay for a while longer and shoot a few hoops."

Ah. Always the gentleman. He was giving her time alone, some breathing room to regain her composure. No wonder everyone in this town acted like he'd hung the moon. The man constantly thought of others.

Darn him. How was she supposed to ignore him if he insisted on being such a good guy?

"Have fun." She turned and was heading toward the house when she found herself adding, "And thanks for the—"

Eek. She slammed her mouth shut. Good grief.

What in the world had she been about to thank him for? He seemed curious about that as well since he stood watching her with an expression that could only be described as cautious and amused.

"Thanks for?" he prompted when she didn't say anything after a few seconds.

Emma scanned her mind, searching for a suitable alternative to thanking him for the best kiss of her life. Finally, she grabbed on to the obvious.

"Thanks for the place to stay. I really appreciate it."

A slow smile crossed his lips, and Emma felt her heart rate accelerate. He knew she hadn't intended on saying that, but he let it go.

"You're welcome," he said, his gaze tangled up with hers. He looked away first, turning slightly and tossing the basketball toward the hoop.

It missed. By several feet. Looked like she wasn't the only one rattled by that kiss.

※

"I DON'T SEE HOW WE CAN HAVE SIMPLIFY READY IN time," said Tim Rollins, Barrett Software's head of testing. "My team keeps finding errors."

"With the voice recognition software?" Nathan asked.

"Yes. Plus, the customizable database doesn't work," Tim explained.

"It works. It just needs some tweaking. We can take care of all of these problems."

This came from Sadie Isles, the head of development.

Nathan held back a sigh and studied the people in the room. They were his lead managers, and they were all looking to him for reassurance. Every single one of them.

"We have a little over five weeks until BizExpo. We need to work together to guarantee the product is done and the demo is flawless."

He turned to Tim. "Have you had the developers sit in on your tests so they can see for themselves what's happening?"

Tim shook his head. "Not yet. But I will."

"Good." Now he looked at Sadie. "That should speed things up."

She nodded. "I'll get with Tim after this meeting and work out a plan."

"Good." Nathan glanced around the room, his gaze lingering way too long on Emma. With effort, he made himself look away. If he didn't watch out, instead of thinking about design problems and coding roadblocks, he'd spend all of his time thinking about how great it had been kissing her last night. So, he needed to stop thinking about her.

"Which is probably impossible."

Nathan froze. Had he said that out loud? He scanned the faces of the other people sitting at the conference table. Based on the frowns he was receiving, it looked as if he had.

Ah, jeez. Way to go, Barrett. Convince the staff you're losing your mind. Should do a lot for employee morale.

"What's impossible?" The question came from Tim. "I think having development sit in on the testing will help."

"That's not what I meant," Nathan assured him. When everyone kept waiting for him to explain his comment, he blurted, "It's impossible not to be excited about Simplify."

Absolute silence fell over the room. Finally, Nathan pulled himself together enough to flash his best smile. Thinking on his feet even while sitting down, he decided to use this opportunity for a little pep talk. "I know. Sounds corny and stupid at this point since we still have a lot of problems and obstacles to overcome before we attend BizExpo. But I can't help it, I'm excited. Simplify is great, and it should really put Barrett Software on the map. I'm proud of how everyone has pulled together and is working as a team to make this happen."

By now, several people at the table were smiling back at him. Whew. That had been close.

Nathan stood, anxious to end the meeting. Anxious to get his head examined. "Okay, any more problems I should know about?"

When no one had anything, he headed toward the door. He should go back to his office, but that would require walking with Emma. More importantly, it would require talking to Emma. At the moment, he figured the less time he spent around Emma, the better.

So, when he left the conference room, he walked with Tim to the testing department. He might as well pitch in himself. He could do some testing and think about something other than Emma and that kiss.

And one other thing he intended on doing was to clean out the garage apartment. The sooner he moved Emma out of the house, the better.

He figured that when it came to Emma Montgomery, he needed to avoid her the way a certain superhero avoids Kryptonite.

EMMA PUT HER HANDS ON HER HIPS AND GLANCED around the room. Boxes were piled everywhere in teetering towers. Cleaning this place out would take hours, but when it was done, she'd have a nice little apartment all to herself. As much as she liked that idea, she felt badly about putting Nathan out.

"You sure you don't mind having this stuff moved? I can see if I can rent a place in town," she offered.

Nathan glanced around the crowded living room and shook his head. "Nice try, but no deal. You're going to help me lug all of this junk over to the attic in the house. There's no welching."

"But you could just leave everything here if it weren't for me," she pointed out.

Nathan walked over and opened a large brown and white box. "I'm not even sure what most of this stuff is," he said, turning to look at her.

As always, she felt a skitter of excitement dance across her skin when their gazes met. "Most of it is stuff my mother kept when I was growing up."

Stunned, she looked at the piles and piles of boxes. "This is all childhood memorabilia? What did she do? Save every paper you ever wrote in school?"

Nathan chuckled. "Not exactly. These are awards and trophies."

Awards? Trophies? All of these boxes? He couldn't be serious. "You're joking, right?"

He shook his head and looked more than a trifle embarrassed. "Nope. Almost all of the boxes have school awards in them. That's why I think I'll move them to the attic in the house. Who knows? Someday I may be interested in looking through this stuff. I doubt it, but you never know."

Emma suspected that Nathan had a sentimental streak in him every bit as wide as the one his mother had had. Look at how much this town meant to him.

She walked over and glanced in one of the boxes. Inside were election posters. She pulled one out, studying the picture of a young Nathan.

"You ran for class president?" Without waiting for his answer, she hurried on. "Of course you did. And let me guess—you won, right?"

He shrugged. "It was a long time ago."

The casual way he answered her made her female antennae go up. "Oh, no, wait a minute. You didn't just win, did you? You slaughtered the competition."

"It was a long time ago," he repeated.

Emma laughed. "I'm right, aren't I?"

By small degrees, a smile appeared on his face. "Something like that."

Figured. It figured Nathan would not only win the election, but he'd win it by a landslide. She'd only known the man for a couple of days, and already she knew that whatever he decided to do, he accomplished.

She studied the picture. Even in his teens, Nathan had been gorgeous. There wasn't a trace of adolescent awkwardness in his picture. Emma shuddered to think what her own school picture had looked like at this age. Braces. Bad hair. Bad skin.

Ick.

But Nathan had been cute. The kind of guy who would never have noticed her if they'd gone to high school together.

"Great poster," she said, feeling more than a little defeated. Before she could be tempted to keep the poster, she quickly tucked it back in the box. Moving into this apartment was a way to put some distance between herself and Nathan. The last thing she needed were any photographs of him.

Nathan picked up one of the larger boxes. "I'm going to start carrying these to the attic."

Emma scurried over to open the door for him. "You need to be careful going down the stairs with something that big. You could fall."

Nathan smiled at her over the top of the box. "Thanks, Mom, for the warning. I also promise not to run with sharp objects."

She frowned. "Very cute. Just don't come to me for help if you tumble down those stairs and smash your head wide open."

"How could I come to you for help if my head is smashed open? I'd sort of be committed to staying where I was, wouldn't I?" he teased.

"Fine. But if you do, just know there's nothing I can do for you. I only know CPR, the Heimlich, and how to treat burns. Beyond that, I barely know the basics of first aid, and certainly not how to put Humpty Dumpty together again."

He laughed. "Great. So there'd be nothing you could do for me? Not one thing?"

Kiss it and make it better? The thought popped into Emma's mind before she braced herself, and she found herself blushing. Really, really blushing. Just like that. One second, she'd been standing there talking to Nathan; the next second, she'd turned bright red. She didn't have to see her face to know what she looked like. She could feel the heat of the blush and wanted the floor to open up and swallow her.

Nathan looked concerned. "Hey, are you okay? You seem...overheated."

Overheated. Yeah. That pretty much described her condition.

Emma willed herself to calm down. When she finally felt she had at least a little control, she said, "I'm fine. Just a little warm."

He looked dubious. "You sure?"

"Absolutely." She moved away from him before she did anything else stupid, and eventually, Nathan either decided to believe her or he lost interest in the subject because he headed out the door and down the stairs.

"Way to go," she muttered to herself. "Act like a complete idiot in front of the man. Who blushes at your age?"

Things were already awkward between them since that blistering kiss they'd shared. She needed to improve the situation, not make it worse by thinking lecherous thoughts about her boss. She needed to forget the kiss had ever happened. Wipe it from her mind. Thinking about that kiss could get her distracted, and at this point in her life, she needed to be distracted by a man about as much as she needed a bad case of warts.

Focus. She simply needed focus. For starters, she'd focus on getting this apartment emptied out. Heading toward the far corner of the room, she picked up a box and opened it. Trophies. As Nathan had promised, the box was filled with trophies. All sizes and shapes and colors.

She picked one up shaped like a basketball and read the plaque. "To the Honey MVP for Eighth Grade."

Nathan came back through the door. With a grin, he headed over to take the trophy from her hands. "I'd forgotten about this."

Emma nodded toward the box. "I can understand why. It looks like you mugged a trophy salesman." Leaning down, she picked up another trophy. This one was a football player. "Another MVP trophy."

Nathan shrugged. "What can I say? I'm good at sports."

Without meaning to, Emma's brain flashed once more on the kiss. Sports weren't all he was good at. Good grief. There she went again. Thinking about the kiss. *Focus, focus, focus.*

Trying to be as casual as possible, she took a couple of steps away from him. Distance. That's what she needed. Lots and lots of distance. And plenty of focus. Focus and distance. Distance and focus.

"Um, Emma?"

She turned and looked at Nathan. "Yes?"

"Are you okay?"

She thought she was, but based on his tone, she guessed not. Looking down, she realized the problem.

She was strangling the trophy she held. Literally strangling the poor football player. "Oops. Sorry."

She carefully replaced the trophy in the box. "Why don't you display these?" she asked, hoping to get her thoughts back on track.

Nathan laughed. "I'd feel like a jerk, to tell you the truth. These are from when I was a kid. A lot of them don't mean anything. Everyone got a trophy."

"Everyone got an MVP trophy in eighth grade? I don't think so. I was in the eighth grade, and I didn't get anything except a broken leg jumping over hurdles in Mrs. Delamaggio's PE class."

She'd been trying to lessen the sexual awareness crackling between them, but her plan backfired. At the mention of her injury, Nathan's gaze shifted to her legs. Just for a second. Maybe only a fraction of a second. But it was long enough for her heart to do a thumpy-thump dance. When his gaze returned to meet hers, she could clearly see desire in his blue eyes. He wanted to kiss her again.

Just as she wanted to kiss him again. For a split second, they stood still, looking at each other. Then, almost as if choreographed, they took giant steps away from each other.

Boy, this was awkward. She could sense Nathan looking at her, but she refused to meet his gaze.

Things between them were getting worse instead of better.

"Hey, anyone up there?"

Relieved to hear the sound of someone else, Emma turned toward the open front door. Nathan crossed the room and looked down the stairs. "Yeah, get on up here and give us a hand."

From the thundering noise coming up the stairs, Emma figured an army was approaching. But after a couple of seconds, a dark-haired man walked through the door.

He flashed a grin, and Emma immediately recognized the man from the pictures she'd seen on the mantel.

"Emma, this is my younger brother, Trent," Nathan said.

Trent crossed the room and shook her hand. "Nice to meet you. You're the friend Leigh brought back from Austin, right?"

Emma nodded, instantly liking the youngest Barrett brother. "Right. I'm working for Nathan for the summer."

Trent turned to Nathan and raised one brow. "Is that a fact? Well, good luck to you then." After glancing around the apartment, he asked, "So what's he got you doing? Helping him move the Nathan Memorial Shrine?"

Nathan groaned. "Cut it out."

Trent's grin only grew bigger. Leaning toward Emma, he said, "Don't let that pretend modesty fool you. Nathan loves each and every prize in this collection Mom assembled for him."

"Did she collect all of your awards as well?" Emma asked. But even before she'd completely finished speaking, both brothers laughed. "What?"

Nathan recovered first. "Trent wasn't exactly what you'd call a model kid growing up."

That surprised Emma. She studied Trent. He had on a police officer's uniform. "Then isn't being on the police force an interesting career choice?"

Trent shrugged. "I'm the chief now, and let's just say, I mended my ways."

From the devious nature of Trent's grin, Emma wasn't one hundred percent certain he'd completely mended his ways. She had the feeling that a few mischievous holes still existed in the man's soul.

Turning back toward Nathan, Trent asked, "Man, you look like executive roadkill." He winked at Emma. "Doesn't Nathan look like hell, Emma? The man's a heart attack waiting to happen."

Nathan frowned at Trent. "Very funny. Why are you here?"

"You're such a charmer, Nathan. Well, since you asked so nicely, I'll nicely answer. I heard Leigh had brought a visitor home from college, so I wanted to stop by and meet her." Trent smiled again at Emma.

Nathan was frowning at his brother. "Okay, you've met her. You going to help us or simply stand there using up oxygen?"

Emma bit back a smile at Nathan's comment. Trent wasn't the least offended. He nudged the closest box with his foot. "Are you sure you're ready to put this shrine into storage?"

"More than sure," Nathan said dryly.

Emma believed him. Although she knew Nathan had worked hard for all these accolades, they seemed to embarrass him.

"Well, if you're sure." Trent picked up one of the boxes. "Where am I carrying this?"

"Attic. And for Emma's sake, be careful not to fall down the stairs. Me, I don't care one way or the other."

Trent nodded, grinned again at Emma, then headed out the door. As he clumped down the stairs, he started whistling. It took a moment for Emma to recognize the song, but when she did, she laughed. Nathan glanced at her. "What?"

"Trent. He's whistling, 'I'm Too Sexy.'"

Nathan made a snorting noise very reminiscent of Leigh's. "In his own mind."

Emma laughed again, then turned her attention back to packing. Carefully, she replaced the trophies, her fingers lingering on Nathan's name carved on one or two. The man certainly had collected more than his share.

Her gaze drifted to the man in question. He was busy packing and taping boxes closed. As he worked, Emma studied him. Now there was a man who was way too sexy; at least, he was too sexy for her own peace of mind.

The thunderous sound of Trent bounding back up the stairs pulled her attention away from Nathan.

"Hey, I forgot to ask you," Trent said as soon as he came through the open door. "Have you heard who Leigh is dating? I can't believe it. Two seconds after Chase leaves on his honeymoon, and she's running around with Jared Kendrick. Have you talked to her yet?"

Nathan shook his head. "No. Not yet."

"Well, one of us needs to and soon." He picked up another box.

Emma couldn't resist pointing out again, "I think

you should let Leigh decide who she wants to date. She's an adult."

Both brothers turned to look at her, their expressions almost identical. They were obviously horrified by her suggestion.

"You don't know Jared," Nathan finally said.

"But I know Leigh. She's smart. And savvy. She wouldn't date this man if he were as terrible as you think. I'm sure he's very nice."

The brothers laughed. "Nice? Jared? Um, not exactly the term I'd use," Nathan said. "The man makes Trent here look like a homebody."

Trent moved over and picked up the box Emma had just finished packing. "I have an idea. I'm taking Sue Ann to the rodeo on Friday night. Emma, why don't you and Nathan come along, and you can meet Jared yourself? I think you'll have a better idea why Nathan and I aren't too pleased about this."

"Who's Sue Ann?" Nathan asked.

Trent groaned. "Sue Ann. You know, the woman I'm dating."

Nathan looked puzzled. "Since when?"

"Nathan, you should be ashamed of yourself. I've been dating Sue Ann for almost a lifetime, and you don't even know her name?"

It did seem kind of remiss to Emma. "I'd love to come to the rodeo. I've never been to one."

"Oh, you'll like it. Lots of fun." Trent headed back toward the door, but Nathan stepped in his way.

"Define a lifetime," Nathan said.

Trent shook his head. "Man, you work too hard.

You're not even current on what's happening with your family. No wonder Leigh's taken up with Jared."

"Define a lifetime," Nathan repeated.

"I've been dating Sue Ann for almost two weeks." Trent nudged by his brother. "You need to get out more."

With that, Trent headed down the stairs.

"He considers two weeks a lifetime?" Emma couldn't help asking.

"Yes. Trent's dating life runs on hyperdrive. He doesn't date any one woman for very long. The last I knew, he was dating a woman named Wendy."

"I guess we'll both get to meet Sue Ann at the same time," Emma said.

Nathan shook his head. "Don't count on it. Friday's a long way away. Trent may be dating someone else by then."

"Those poor women," Emma said, shaking her head slowly.

"No, they know what Trent's like. None of them take him seriously. He's a flirt, good for a few laughs, a little fun. But he's not the type to settle down. The ladies in this town know what kind of guy he is," Nathan assured her. "Trent doesn't go out with women who don't look at romance the same way he does."

For one split second, Emma almost asked Nathan what kind of guy he was. But then she realized she already knew. Nathan was the forever kind. When he fell in love, he'd always stay in love. He'd settle in this town that adored him and live happily ever after with a no-doubt absolutely perfect wife who would be gorgeous and smart and funny and didn't need to constantly eat antacids to keep the bubbling in her stomach under control just because she was trying her darnedest to work on a doctoral thesis that didn't want to cooperate no matter what she tried and—

"You okay?" Nathan asked once again.

Emma blinked. Good grief. Where had all that come from? She looked at Nathan. He was frowning at her.

Apparently, she wasn't okay. Apparently, she harbored a great deal of dislike for a woman Nathan hadn't even met yet. How weird was that? It wasn't like she was jealous. The last thing she wanted to do was fall for a man who had roots in a small town like this one. She had her own plans. Her own goals. She didn't want to live happily ever after with Nathan, even if he was a fantastic kisser.

Nathan moved toward her. "Really, are you okay?"

"Um, yeah. I'm fine," she finally managed to say once she remembered how to speak.

Oh, yeah, she was fine all right. Losing her mind. But other than that, right as rain.

Nathan was obviously unconvinced. "Are you sure?"

She could hardly tell him what she'd been thinking, so she settled for saying, "I was worrying about my dissertation."

"Ah." For a moment, he simply studied her and looked as if he might challenge her response. Then, thankfully, he turned and went back to work.

Emma released the breath she'd been holding. Fumbling in her pocket, she pulled out an antacid and chewed it slowly.

Good thing she wasn't sticking around this town for

much longer. Honey was starting to get to her. If she didn't watch herself, pretty soon she'd be gossiping about Leigh and stepping over dogs that looked like they hadn't moved in a couple of years and sneaking into Nathan's office to do cheers.

Yep, it was a really good thing she was leaving in five weeks. A really good thing

5

"Hey, where are you hiding, Emma?" Leigh asked, waltzing into the family room like it wasn't almost two in the morning.

Nathan nodded toward the grandfather clock in the corner. "Kinda late, isn't it?"

Leigh flopped onto the sofa. "You're too young to be so old."

"Ha, very funny." Turning his options over in his mind, Nathan chose his words carefully. Yelling at Leigh wouldn't do any good. As Emma kept pointing out, his sister was an adult. A wild adult, but still an adult. So all he said was, "I worry about you, Leigh. I don't want you to get hurt."

She groaned. "I'm a grown woman. You and Trent and Chase have to accept it."

His gut instinct was to argue with her, but Leigh was right. He had to let her make her own choices in life even if those choices made him crazy. It was so damn difficult not to worry about Leigh. She might be an adult, but she also attracted trouble like a picnic attracted ants.

"I'll butt out if you promise me you'll be careful," he finally said.

Leigh flashed him a grin. "Wow, Nathan, that's quite a concession from you. I can't believe it."

"Yeah, well, just so you know, I'm not too happy about it, either. Don't make me regret this, okay? That means, I'm not going to step in and save you, either, so be very careful what you do."

She drew an imaginary X on her chest. "I promise. I won't get in trouble."

"Why don't I believe that?"

"Because you're a cynic."

No, it was because he knew his sister. But as difficult as it was going to be, Nathan vowed he'd stand by his agreement. He'd butt out of her life, even if it drove him insane.

Leigh settled back on the couch, looking way too pleased with herself. "So, you never told me what you did with Emma."

"She moved into the garage apartment," he said. "And Trent and I really appreciate all the help you gave us."

Leigh laughed. "You're cute when you're snotty. Seriously, I would have helped. If I'd known."

"I told you twice that Emma and I were cleaning out the apartment after work."

Leigh pretended to consider what he said. "Oh, you mean when you called this afternoon and said 'Leigh, we're cleaning out the apartment after work' you meant you were—"

"Cleaning out the apartment after work," he said dryly.

"Ah. Well, that explains why I got confused. You need to be clearer when you tell me these things, Nathan. Jeez, I'm not a mind reader."

"Funny. Very funny. Seriously, you should spend at least a little time with Emma. You did convince her to come to Honey."

Leigh narrowed her eyes. "Are you getting tired of her company?"

His sister was being annoying, and she knew it. "I don't think you're being a very good friend, that's all."

"Ouch. Got me with that one. Okay, I'll spend more time with Emma." Her expression brightened. "I know, I'll ask her to come to the rodeo with me."

"Trent already did," Nathan pointed out.

Leigh blinked. "Excuse me?"

"He's taking his latest girlfriend to the rodeo on Friday and asked Emma to come along."

"Trent's taking Emma along on one of his dates?" Leigh's laughter bubbled out. "Now that I'd like to see. Emma, playing chaperone."

"I'm going with them, so it won't be like Emma's a third wheel."

The grin on Leigh's face turned downright mischievous. "Oh, really? You're going along? What, as Emma's date?"

Nathan frowned, not appreciating his sister's sense of humor in the least. "Of course not." "Why not? I know you like Emma."

"She works for me, in case you've forgotten," Nathan said pointedly, hoping Leigh would get the hint and drop the subject. But true to form, the more sensitive the topic, the more it interested Leigh.

"Is that the best excuse you can come up with?" Leigh asked with a snort. "If you like Emma, you should go ahead and date her."

"I have no interest in dating Emma," Nathan maintained, knowing that he was lying like a rug. Lying badly, too. But the last person he wanted to discuss Emma with was Leigh. "I simply thought she might be more comfortable going to the rodeo if I came along, too."

Leigh clearly didn't buy his excuse for a second. "Seriously, why don't you go out with Emma? I think the two of you would be perfect together."

Suspicion slammed into Nathan. He hadn't been born yesterday, and he could smell one of Leigh's plots a mile away. Not that this one was proving to be much of a challenge. His sister's intentions had been fairly obvious all along.

"Leigh, I know your plan is to try to fix me up with Emma."

She fluttered her eyelashes. "Who, me? Never."

Nathan ignored her denial and continued, "It isn't going to work. Emma and I are too different, and we both have our own agendas and things we want to achieve. It would never work out between us, so stop being a pest."

"That's a nice little speech. Who are you trying to convince—you or me?"

Nathan sighed. Today had been a really long day, and the last thing he wanted to do was discuss Emma with Leigh. Truthfully, he didn't want to think about Emma at all. He'd done way too much of that today as it was.

"Why don't we spend a little time talking about you and Jared? Seems to me you two are spending way too much time together."

Leigh laughed. "Nice way to turn the tables, big brother. Okay, if you want to talk about Jared, we will. He and I have gone out on a couple of dates. Nothing serious, and it's no big deal."

It took every ounce of Nathan's self-control not to point out to his sister that Jared was hardly the right sort of man for her to be dating. Leigh knew very well what sort Jared was, and he'd promised to back off. But promising and doing were two very different things.

"You know I'm worried about you?" was all he finally said.

Leigh crossed the room and gave him a big hug. "Yes. And you're sweet to be that way. A total pain in the rear, of course. But sweet."

Nathan chuckled. "Thanks. I think."

"So, here's the deal. I'll butt out of your love life, and you'll butt out of mine. That way we'll both have only ourselves to blame no matter how things turn out."

Since Nathan would give anything to keep Leigh from meddling in his love life, he accepted the agreement. He wasn't happy about it because he really felt she was making a huge mistake by going out with Jared. But he accepted it.

"Deal," he reluctantly said.

Leigh hugged him again and gave him a loud, smacking kiss on his cheek. "Did I ever tell you that you're my favorite brother?"

"You're a natural born con artist, kiddo."

"It's a talent, what can I say?"

Nathan couldn't help laughing. His sister drove him nuts and worried him sick. She also made his life a lot of fun. He wanted the very best for her. "Promise you'll be careful," he said.

Leigh sighed. "You know, I'm not the only one who should be worried about winding up with a broken heart. You could be in trouble and not even know it."

Nathan wanted to argue but couldn't. When the lady had a point, she had a point.

❧

"ARE ALL RODEOS THIS NOISY?" EMMA ASKED, LEANING closer to Nathan.

He grinned. "If they're done right, they are. Why, is it getting to you?"

Emma shook her head. No. The noise wasn't bothering her. Not really. In fact, for the most part, she found the experience exhilarating. It was hard to believe she'd lived in Texas so long and hadn't once gone to a rodeo. But up until tonight, she'd never imagined she'd have fun at a rodeo.

Of course, she'd never been to one with Nathan before.

"The man on the horse is Jared," Nathan said, indicating a tall rider in the main arena. "That means Leigh's probably around somewhere nearby."

Emma scanned the crowd, finally spotting Leigh on the far side. "She's right there."

Nathan nodded. "See. I knew she'd be nearby. She can no more resist Jared than a bird can resist a freshly washed car."

His tone was resigned, but Emma didn't buy Nathan's act for a minute. He didn't like Leigh dating this Jared person, but he was trying to be civilized about the situation. On her other side, Trent had no such reluctance. He'd kept up a running soliloquy for the past half hour about how his sister was involved with the wrong guy.

Not that Trent's date seemed to be his soul mate. As far as Emma could tell, Sue Ann Finely had ogled every man in the place. Twice. The petite redhead wasn't exactly subtle, either. She'd even oohed and aahed a couple of times and once leaned over Trent to nudge Emma and say, "Check out the guy in the white Stetson."

No, Trent and Sue Ann weren't a love match. Trent was equally unfocused on his date. If he wasn't complaining about Jared, he was smiling at the women who stopped by to say hi to one or both of the Barrett brothers.

Emma was finding the show in the stands much more interesting than anything happening in the arena. Six women had already stopped by specifically to say hello to Nathan. Caitlin Estes had stopped by twice. And each time, Emma made herself ignore any inappropriate feelings she might have toward the women flirting with Nathan. It wasn't any of her business, and she certainly wasn't jealous. Nathan was her boss, and hopefully, her friend. But that was all.

And she reminded herself of that each time one of those hussies...er, um, ladies stopped by to say hello.

Trent hollered across Emma to get his brother's attention. "Hey, Nathan, maybe we'll luck out and Jared will disappear like he did before, then our problems are solved."

"Don't be a meanie," Sue Ann said. "Jared's a great guy."

Both Trent and Nathan snorted in unison, and Emma bit back a smile. These Barretts certainly weren't shy about letting the world know their opinions.

"Great is a relative term, Sue Ann," Nathan muttered.

Sue Ann frowned. "He's not my relative. I just like him."

"That's not what I meant," Nathan started. "I meant that not everyone thinks he's great."

Sue Ann turned in her seat so she could half face Nathan. The movement made her oversize silver earrings sway and bob, and Emma once more found herself wondering why a woman as tiny as Sue Ann would want to wear earrings the size of grapefruit.

They kept clinking and clanking. Just like the rodeo, Sue Ann's earrings were making a lot of noise.

"Well, whatever you meant, you're wrong about Jared. He is great. And trust me, I should know. I used to date a rodeo clown," Sue Ann announced. Then she settled back in her seat as if she'd somehow ended the argument.

Nathan glanced at Emma, a baffled expression on his face. "What?"

Emma shrugged. "Beats me."

Before any of them could ask Sue Ann to explain, she stood, straightened her T-shirt that read *Everything is Bigger in Texas*, and said, "Y'all please excuse me while I go to the little girls' room."

Nathan had a definite twinkle in his eyes when after Sue Ann left, he leaned toward Emma and asked, "You want to ask about the rodeo clown, or should I?"

"You ask." Emma took a sip of her soda. "I'm happy pretending I know what she's talking about."

Nathan sighed with exaggerated dramatic flair. "Fine. I'll ask." He looked at his brother. "I don't suppose you know what Sue Ann meant. I mean, you have been dating the woman for a lifetime."

Trent shook his head. "Haven't a clue. But Sue Ann is like that. Full of mystery. I prefer to remain unenlightened most of the time."

Emma turned to look at him. "Trent, how can you build a relationship with someone when you don't make an effort to understand them?"

Trent scratched the side of his face. "Relationship? Let me think here for a second." He snapped his fingers and grinned. "That's right. I'm not worried about my relationship with Sue Ann because we don't have a relationship. We're just dating."

A loud cheer went up from the crowd, momentarily distracting Emma. Jared must have done something good in the rodeo world, but Emma hadn't a clue what it was, so she turned her attention back to Trent just as Sue Ann returned from the restroom.

"Still, I think when two people are dating, they should understand each other. Know how the other one feels about a lot of subjects. It's not enough simply to share common interests. You should know a great deal about the other person."

Sue Ann settled back into her seat, gave Trent a

loud, smacking kiss, then looked at Emma. "What sort of things should you know?"

Emma shrugged. "Well, for starters, there's the usual. Where each of you went to school. Your birthday. Things about your family. Your goals and dreams. Then you should also learn each other's philosophies and ideologies."

Sue Ann blinked. Twice. "Why would I need to know all that? We're just dating."

Emma couldn't believe they were having this conversation. It seemed to her this was obvious. "Aren't you curious about the person you're dating?"

Sue Ann grinned. "Oh, honey. I know plenty about Trent. Plenty." Then she proceeded to give Trent a couple more smacky kisses.

Emma was all set to continue her debate with Sue Ann and Trent as soon as they came up for air, but Nathan patted her on the arm. "You might as well let it go. They're not going to see this your way. Trent doesn't do relationships, and he doesn't date women who do relationships."

With a sigh, Emma settled back in her seat. "I just don't understand. How can they not know at least the fundamentals, like each other's birthdays?"

"Different approaches to life, I guess."

"It's not like the two of you know each other's birthdays, either," Trent said, draping an arm around Sue Ann.

"Emma and I aren't dating—"

"October seven," Emma said without thinking. Nathan turned and looked at her, surprise evident on his handsome face. "You know when my birthday is?

Why?"

"Your previous assistant had it marked on the calendar," Emma confessed, feeling like a fool for offering up the information. Now both Trent and Sue Ann were grinning at her as if she'd let slip some great state secret.

"So, Nathan," Trent said slowly. "I don't suppose there's any chance you know when Emma's birthday is?"

"That really doesn't prove anything, so wipe that stupid smirk off your face," Nathan said.

Sue Ann looked from Emma to Nathan then back at Emma. "Does that mean he knows?"

Truthfully, Emma wasn't sure. She also wasn't sure that she wanted to know if he knew.

"It doesn't matter," she hurriedly said, wanting to direct the conversation in a new—and hopefully not so dangerous—direction. "All I was trying to say was that it seems to me that people who are dating would want to share information about themselves."

Sue Ann leaned across Trent and yelled to Nathan, "Hey, do you know when her birthday is or not? You never did answer my question."

Nathan frowned. "Emma's point is that—"

"I think he knows," Sue Ann announced in a singsong voice. "I think he knows." She looked at Trent. "Seems to me, these two sure talk a lot about being honest and upfront with people, but then they sure are sneaky about some things."

Trent grinned at his brother. "I couldn't agree with you more, Sue Ann. And usually Nathan is such a trustworthy, forthright person. I can't imagine what's gotten into him tonight."

Nathan groaned. "I don't know what I did to deserve you as a brother."

"Stood in the right place at the right time. Seriously, you need me in your life, Nathan. I keep you on your toes. So now, tell me. When's Emma's birthday?"

For a second, Nathan remained silent. Then he said, "November two."

That was the last thing Emma had expected. Stunned, she turned to look at him. "How in the world did you know? I never told you when my birthday was."

"It was on your application. I'm good at remembering numbers."

For several long moments, Emma simply looked at Nathan. She was surprised by his revelation. Truly surprised. Next to her, Trent and Sue Ann laughed and teased, but Emma couldn't focus on their nonsense. All she could focus on was Nathan.

Then another cheer from the crowd broke the spell that had settled over her. She blinked and looked away from Nathan.

"I knew you'd know when her birthday was. You can't fool me," Trent said.

Nathan gave his brother a narrow-eyed look. "Just because I know when her birthday is doesn't mean anything."

"Sure it does."

Emma had to jump in on this one. "No, Trent, it doesn't. As Nathan explained, he's good at remembering numbers and happens to remember when my birthday is. It doesn't mean anything."

"Then why doesn't Trent remember when my

birthday is?" Sue Ann asked with a pout. "I've told him a couple of times, but he keeps forgetting."

"Trent has the manners of a warthog," Nathan explained.

Rather than being offended, Trent laughed again.

"Not true. It's just that while you're good with numbers, I'm the brother who's good with his hands."

"I can swear to that," Sue Ann said with a giggle.

For one stupid nanosecond, Emma wanted to point out that Trent wasn't the only talented Barrett brother. Nathan had fogged her windows when he'd kissed her. But thankfully, before she could say something that would embarrass both her and Nathan, common sense returned, and she kept her mouth shut. The last thing she wanted to do was fuel any errant speculation.

But boy oh boy, was she tempted.

❦

"Did you enjoy the rodeo?" Nathan asked on the drive home.

So far, Emma had been pretty silent. Not that he'd set any records for conversation himself, but still, the silence in the car was starting to be awkward.

Of course, that wasn't what was bothering him the most. What bothered him more was the reason that the silence was awkward. He was way too aware of Emma sitting next to him. All evening, he'd been at war with himself, wanting to kiss her, to touch her again.

How stupid could he be?

Apparently very stupid since despite his best efforts, he couldn't stop thinking about kissing her. So now he was hoping if he could get Emma talking, it would take his mind off all the other things he had no darn business thinking about. Like how great it felt to hold her. And touch her. And kiss her.

"The rodeo was interesting," she said. "But I wish I'd had a chance to talk to Leigh. I haven't seen much of her since I came to Honey. But she obviously had a great time. She seemed so excited tonight at the rodeo."

"When the words Leigh and excited end up in a sentence together, bad things usually happen," Nathan said dryly.

Emma laughed. "Oh, come on, your sister isn't that bad."

Nathan couldn't help asking, "Are you certain you've actually met my sister? Because if you have, I can't believe you'd say that."

"I'll admit, she has a different approach to life. But she's smart and fun and determined."

Nathan pulled the car into the driveway and parked it inside the garage. "It's the determined part that worries me. You didn't have a chance to meet Jared tonight, but trust me, he isn't the type to settle down and raise two-point-five children."

"Don't take this the wrong way, because I know Leigh's your sister, but I don't think she's looking for a guy to settle down with."

Emma shifted in her seat, so she was turned toward him. In the bright light in the garage, Nathan could clearly see her face. She smiled slowly, and lust slammed into him. She was so pretty, so sweet and smart. No matter what his brain told him about not being attracted to her, his body had tuned him out.

Almost against his will, he reached out and brushed a couple of strands of hair away from her eyes. Emma seemed surprised by his action, but she didn't pull back.

"What about you? Are you looking for two-point-five children?" he asked, then wanted to hit himself in the head with a laptop when he did. What was wrong with him? He shouldn't be touching Emma's soft hair. Nor should he be flirting with her.

"Sorry about that. I shouldn't have touched you. I apologize," he said, meaning it. She worked for him. He wanted her to know he wasn't trying something.

"Nathan, it's fine," she said.

"I also shouldn't pry into your personal life," he said.

"Nathan, is this because I work for you?"

"Yes. I want you to know—"

She waved a hand. "I know you would never use your position as my boss to your advantage. I also know you would not use your position as my temporary non-paid landlord. I don't feel any obligation to repay you in any way." She smiled and added, "You are not pressuring me in any way, so please don't worry."

Emma opened her car door and climbed out. Nathan reluctantly did the same.

"Now, to answer your question, I'm too busy right now to think about things like a family," she said, shutting her car door. The metallic click the door made seemed to add an auditory emphasis to her statement. "After all these years, I'm finally going to get my doctorate. I'm also going to have a chance to spend time with my father. My future is mapped out."

Nathan nodded and waited for her to precede him

out of the garage. "I wasn't talking about right now. I know you've got plans. I meant later."

Emma stopped at the bottom of the stairs leading to the garage apartment. She turned her head to look at him. "I haven't really thought about it. I was an only child who was raised to act more like an adult than like a child. I don't know much about children. I don't even know if I'd make a good mother."

"Of course, you would." He moved closer to her. "Look at how patient you are with Leigh."

Emma laughed softly, the sound enticing in the still night air. "You love your sister, and you know it."

"Yeah, I do," he admitted. He nodded toward the top of the stairs. "My mother raised me too well not to walk you to your door."

"You're kidding, right? I'm what? Fifteen steps from the top?"

"If you'd known my mom, you'd understand why I have to do this."

Emma rolled her eyes, but her smile made it clear she didn't object. "Fine. Far be it from me to undo a mother's training."

She preceded him up the steps, stopping once or twice to glance around and say, "See any monsters yet? Any robbers?"

Nathan simply sighed and continued to follow her. But when they reached the landing and Emma opened the door, he realized immediately that he'd had an ulterior motive all along. Because the second she opened that door, he followed her inside the apartment without once considering the consequences.

"See, I'm safely home," she said, turning on the

small lamp by the door. "Thanks again for taking me to the rodeo. It was fun."

The atmosphere between them seemed to crackle. He should never have followed her up the stairs. He should have stayed downstairs, far away from her.

Far away from temptation. But all of the IQ tests he'd taken in school were dead wrong about him—he wasn't smart. He wasn't even marginally bright.

He was the stupidest man to ever draw a breath because on the landing, she gave him a flirty smile and kissed him.

Even knowing he shouldn't, he leaned forward and kissed Emma back.

✤ 6 ✤

Emma was glad he kissed her back. She'd wanted Nathan to kiss her since the last time on the basketball court. So here she was, getting her wish.

Without questioning her good fortune, when Nathan slid his tongue across her bottom lip, Emma opened her mouth, rose up on her toes, and slipped her arms around his neck. He instantly accepted the offer she made, wrapping his strong arms around her and settling her body intimately against him. Then his tongue met hers in a slow, seductive dance.

Yahoo.

Instinctively, Emma pressed harder against him. He sure could kiss. She felt him everywhere, heat flooding through her. Maybe someday she'd be embarrassed that she'd acted this way, but not tonight. Tonight, she wanted this kiss to go on forever.

He turned her slightly and backed her against the door. Then he cupped her upturned face as he deepened the kiss. Emma was lost in the wonder of his embrace when the sound of a car engine coming up the driveway finally seeped through her lust-fogged brain.

Nathan heard it, too, and he ended the kiss and leaned his forehead against hers.

"Leigh is home," he said finally, his voice husky.

It took a minute for his meaning to dawn on Emma, but when it did, she slipped out of his embrace and hurriedly put the distance of the small living room between them. Leigh was home from her date, and the last thing Emma wanted was for her friend to find her kissing Nathan.

Truthfully, calling what they'd just been doing kissing was like calling a tornado a gentle breeze. They'd been on fire, and it was going to take some doing for her to get her pulse rate under control.

Nathan didn't seem to be doing much better. Unfulfilled desire still heated his gaze, and his breathing was rapid and ragged.

"I should leave," he said.

Emma nodded. "Probably the best idea."

But he didn't leave. He stood looking at her. He seemed as consumed by indecision as she was. They both knew the right thing for him to do was to leave. But a part of Emma, a really nosy, annoying part, couldn't help wishing he'd forget about doing the smart thing and instead cross the room and kiss her crazy once more.

But Nathan didn't move. Instead, he remained across the room from her and said, "We need to stop kissing like that."

Before Emma could stop herself, she asked, "How would you like to kiss?"

Nathan tipped his head and gave her a mischievous look. "You know what I mean."

Yes, she did. Unfortunately.

"What do you suggest? I mean, we both already agreed not to kiss again, and yet we did," she pointed out.

"True." Nathan leaned against the door, obviously lost in thought. Emma waited patiently for any suggestion he might have. She certainly didn't have one of her own to offer. She wanted Nathan. A lot. And even though getting involved with him would mess up her plans, she couldn't seem to get her brain to win the war it was fighting with her traitorous body.

"Do you have any suggestions?" Nathan asked.

Give in to temptation was the first thought to cross her mind.

Okay, bad idea.

"Let me think." But the longer she thought, the fewer ideas came to her. She couldn't afford to lose any money, and she also wasn't completely sure that she wouldn't kiss Nathan again. So that meant that whatever punishment they thought of couldn't be too terrible. Just on the off chance she lost the wager, of course.

An idea eventually occurred to her. "How about the loser washes the winner's car?"

"Which one is considered the loser, and which one is considered the winner?"

She frowned. "Whoever kisses the other first has to wash the other person's car."

Nathan looked openly dubious. "You think that's a strong enough incentive to keep us from kissing?"

"It's the best I can think of. Unless you have a better idea."

"No," he said. "Okay, that will be our penalty." He opened the door. "Leigh's already inside, so I'm going to head on home. Talk to you tomorrow."

"See you."

Right before he shut the door he said, "For the record, I have a feeling that before this summer is over, we'll both end up with really clean cars." Funny, she had the exact same feeling.

"YOUNG MAN, DO YOU HAVE ANY IDEA HOW LATE IT is?" Leigh teased the second Nathan walked into the kitchen. "Have you been hanging out with floozies and ne'er-do-wells?"

Great. Just great. He should have expected his sister to ambush him.

"You haven't been home long yourself," he pointed out.

She laughed. "True, but then, I was with a ne'er-do-well, which means you must have been with a floozy."

"Very funny."

"Seriously, didn't you just leave Emma's apartment?" She gave him a wicked grin. "Anything happen I should know about? Do I need to clear my calendar and make room for another wedding?"

Although Nathan knew Leigh was only kidding, he couldn't stop himself from glaring at her.

"For your information, I walked Emma to her apartment door when we got home from the rodeo. It's that simple, so don't make a big deal out of this." He walked past her and got a soda out of the refrigerator. Even though it was after midnight, he needed something to help him cool off. The kiss he'd shared with Emma still had his blood simmering.

Leigh leaned against the counter and crossed her arms over her chest. Nathan could almost see the gears grinding in her devious mind, and he decided to head her off before she started plotting and planning.

"How about you? Should I start dusting off my tux for a wedding between you and Jared?"

Leigh laughed. "As if. And you know it. So is this your way of telling me to mind my own business?"

"Yes," he admitted.

For a couple of seconds, Leigh studied him. Just when Nathan had given up hope, she shrugged.

"Fine by me. Don't tell me what's up between you and Emma. I won't pry. But you were the one who pointed out to me that Emma is a woman who's got her life mapped out and is probably not the right woman for you. I'm only reminding you because I don't want to see you get hurt when she leaves."

The warning seemed ridiculous coming from Leigh. She was the one in danger of getting hurt, not him. Still, he appreciated the thought behind her concern.

"I have nothing to worry about, Leigh. I already told you, I'm not getting involved with Emma."

"Whatever you say," she said. "But for the record, I look best in bridesmaid gowns that are burgundy, blue, or green. Whatever happens, I do not want to be stuck in a yellow gown. I look like a giant french fry. Got it?"

Nathan frowned. "Go to bed, Leigh."

"Okey dokey." Laughing, his sister headed up the back stairs. But long after she went to bed, Nathan sat in his study, wondering what in the world he was going to do about this attraction he felt for Emma. Not only were they all wrong for each other, but now wasn't the time to let himself get distracted. He couldn't get involved with a woman right now. Maybe after BizExpo. Maybe after Simplify became a success.

But not now.

And besides, it wasn't like he could build a future with Emma. In five weeks she was returning to Austin and then moving to Massachusetts. The best they could hope for was a fling. Is that really what he wanted at this point in his life? He was too old not to think about the future.

And much too old to be acting like a lust-crazed teenager. So, the best approach would be to only see Emma at work. He'd make certain he didn't spend time with her outside the office. That way he wouldn't be tempted to touch her or kiss her again.

Okay, maybe he'd be tempted, but he wouldn't be able to act on that temptation. And at this point, he'd settle for what he could get.

Avoidance. That was the key. He had to avoid Emma at all costs. He wouldn't get caught within twenty feet of the woman.

"IT'S REALLY NICE OF YOU TO INVITE ME TO YOUR brother's house for dinner," Emma said two days later as she sat in the passenger seat of Nathan's luxury sedan.

"Ha, like he had a choice," Leigh said with a snort from the back seat. "Megan and Chase want to meet you. He was told to bring us both to dinner. No arguments."

Emma turned and looked at her friend. "Still, it's nice of Nathan to drive."

Again, Leigh snorted. "You're thanking him for nothing. He's one of those guys who always drives. Always. He's got that have-to-be-in-control thing that prevents him from letting someone else take over." She tapped her brother on the shoulder. "Isn't that right, Nathan?"

"Huh? Are you talking to me? I thought you were going to just talk about me the whole drive without once acknowledging that I'm sitting right here. I was worried for a second that I'd gone invisible."

Leigh laughed, and Emma couldn't help smiling at Nathan's good-natured teasing.

"You're such a jerk," Leigh said, laughter still tinting her voice. "Seriously, tell Emma how you always like to be in charge."

"I only like to be in charge, Leigh, because I'm always right about things."

Emma had to laugh now. "Oh, please. No one is always right. Everyone is occasionally wrong."

"Even you?" Leigh teased. "I thought you were always right."

"Hyperbole."

"Not Nathan," Leigh said from the back seat. "I

can't think of a single time when he's been wrong. It really fries my hush puppies, but it's true."

That was ridiculous and couldn't possibly be accurate. "He wouldn't be human if he didn't make mistakes," Emma said. And she, of all people, knew that Nathan was human. Boy oh boy, did she ever. The man was definitely flesh and blood and kisses hot enough to make her toes curl.

Just the thought of the last kiss they'd shared distracted her to the point where it took a couple of seconds for her to realize Leigh was talking to her.

"...so when the weather people said it wasn't going to rain, Daddy told Nathan he was about to be proven wrong. But it didn't rain. It poured. It deluged. Just like Nathan said it would. So even as a kid, he was never wrong."

Although Emma had missed the first part of Leigh's story, she'd heard enough to get the gist of it.

"That's an educated guess," Emma said. She shifted in her seat to look at Nathan. He seemed highly amused by the entire conversation. No doubt his ego was feeling pretty well fed with his sister singing his praises this way.

But come on! Never wrong? It was impossible.

And blatantly untrue. Two nights ago, when he'd kissed her, he'd been wrong. They both had agreed not to kiss anymore, and yet, Nathan had broken that promise. He'd kissed her. Okay, so she had started it, but he had kissed her back.

But that was an example she couldn't share with Leigh.

"And then there's Rufus," Leigh went on. "Last year,

everyone said there was no way to get that dog into a car and take him to the vet. His owner, Steve Myerson, was frantic. Honey doesn't have its own vet, so Rufus has to be driven to where there is one. Nathan finally got involved and solved the problem."

Despite herself, Emma had to know. "What did you do?" she asked Nathan.

"Nothing special." Nathan turned the car down a long, narrow driveway leading to what looked like a pretty, white house.

"Double ha," Leigh said. "He knew right away what would work. And he was right. The dog has a thing for bright-pink tennis balls. Not white or yellow. The ball has to be pink. But if you throw one, he will follow. Well, sort of. As much as Rufus follows anything. Somehow, Nathan knew it would work."

"You're able to read the minds of dogs?" Emma teased. "Wow, now there's a skill that could come in handy. Met any talking horses? Chickens with a lot on their minds? Interesting cows?"

Nathan chuckled, the sound rich and deep. Without trying, she could remember every detail of his last kiss. The way he'd held her in his arms. The way his mouth had felt against her own. The way—

Stop it!

Emma mentally kicked herself. Enough of that. She was not going to think about kissing Nathan again. Thinking about him was bad for her health. At least for her mental health. He should come with a big warning label slapped on his side that said: Contact with Lonely Women Can Result in a Loss of Intelligence.

Because that was the problem with kissing Nathan

—it confused her. A lot. Every time she kissed him, she lost all sense of priority. Up until meeting Nathan, she'd always thought she had the willpower of three people. Now she knew that when really tempted, she caved quicker than a sandcastle hit by a wave.

Not that it was entirely her fault, though. The man was gorgeous and smart and nice and one heck of a kisser. Plus, when he took off his shirt to play basketball, the sun gleamed across his strong muscles and—

"Yoo-hoo, Emma?" Leigh said from behind her. "You still with us, or have you been secretly kidnapped by aliens who left your body behind? If it's the aliens thing, dibs on selling the story to the tabloids."

Emma blew out a shaky breath. Wow. She really needed to get herself under control. Finally, she managed to ask, "What did you want, Leigh?"

"You're not listening to us. Nathan asked you a question, and you've been sitting there like a zombie," Leigh said.

She had? She was? Good grief. With effort, Emma turned her head and looked at Leigh, her mind still struggling to banish the image she'd conjured up of Nathan without a shirt. Um. What were they talking about? Oh, right. Her losing her mind.

"I'm still here," she said. "Sorry. I was thinking about—" Words failed her. What could she say? She'd been thinking about...

Nathan.

She shook her head and tried again. "Work."

Leigh frowned. "Work? You mean your dissertation?"

Relief flowed through Emma, and she lunged for the

excuse. "Exactly. My dissertation. I was thinking about my dissertation."

Leigh snorted. "As if."

Emma made a snorting noise right back. "It's the truth."

"Yeah right, and I'm the Tooth Fairy."

"Leave her alone," Nathan told his sister, pulling his car up in front of a two-story house.

Leigh held up her hands. "Fine. I won't bother Emma." She opened her door and right before she stepped out, she said to her brother, "But I mean it—no yellow."

"What is she talking about? No yellow what?" Emma looked at Nathan, hoping her errant thoughts had calmed down enough that she wouldn't keep having erotic images of him.

Wrong. One smile from him and her heart took off like a Thoroughbred in an open field. This dinner with Nathan's family was going to be much more difficult than she'd anticipated if she couldn't get her libido under control.

"Are you okay?" Nathan asked.

Oh, no. Not that again. Emma forced a smile across her face, but she knew desire still flickered in her gaze. She could see the answering attraction on Nathan's face. For countless seconds, they simply looked at each other. Then Emma finally managed to say in a way-too-raspy voice, "I'm fine. Truly fine."

Nathan grinned. "Yeah. I know."

"WHAT'S TAKING YOU SO LONG? HURRY UP," TRENT yelled at Nathan.

Nathan headed down the porch steps and crossed over to Chase's garage. As usual following a Sunday dinner, he and Trent were admiring the classic 1956 Pontiac Star Chief Chase was restoring. But this ritual was all that was usual about today. Not a single other thing was the way it normally was. Chase had spent the past two hours flirting and kissing with his new wife, Megan. And Trent had brought yet another new girlfriend to dinner. What was her name? Amber? Autumn? Azalea?

"What's your date's name?" he asked Trent when he rejoined his brothers.

Trent shot a narrowed-eyed look at Nathan. "Azure. Her name is Azure."

"Right. Azure." Nathan watched as Trent ran one hand over the new chrome fender Chase had added in the past week.

"This car is a beauty, Chase," Trent said.

Nathan had to ask, "Trent, what happened to Sue Ann? You seemed pretty happy at the rodeo two nights ago."

Chase turned to look at Trent. "You've changed girlfriends in the past two days? When are you going to learn that the grass isn't greener?"

Trent grinned. "When the grass stops being greener."

"You've got the wrong attitude toward love," Chase said.

"Who's talking about love? I thought we were talking about dating." Trent laughed at his own joke.

"He's going to die alone because he's never going to grow up and become an adult," Chase said to Nathan. "A man needs to settle down at some point in his life."

Nathan couldn't help laughing. "That's what you say now that you're in love with Megan. But if memory serves me, you were kicking and screaming about not falling in love just a few months ago, Chase. You drove Trent and me crazy telling us you didn't believe in love, and there was no way you were in love with Megan."

"I was a fool," Chase said, then he said to Trent, "Hey, stop touching the chrome."

"Jeez, I'm not three, Chase."

Chase looked at Nathan. "He does a pretty good imitation, doesn't he?"

"Funny. Very funny." Trent went back to admiring the car.

Chase moved over to stand next to Trent. "Seriously, marriage is wonderful. A man needs to find a special woman and build a life with her."

Both Nathan and Trent dissolved into laughter.

"What?" Chase asked, looking affronted. "It's true."

"You sound like a greeting card," Trent said.

Chase snorted. "You two are just jealous because I've found someone great, and you'll be lucky to have a buzzard give you a second look."

Boy, Chase's tune sure had changed since he'd married Megan. If ever there'd been a man who was convinced love didn't exist, it had been Chase.

But Megan had changed his mind.

Just thinking about his brother's happy marriage made Nathan wish things were different with Emma. She was unlike any woman he'd ever met. Not only was he attracted to her, but he also loved spending time with her, listening to her, joking with her.

She was one special lady.

"Yo, Nathan. Are you having a stroke or something?" Trent trotted over and slapped him on the back, knocking most of the air right out of Nathan's lungs. "You look weird."

Nathan struggled to regain his breath. "Hey, Trent, you almost killed me."

"I did not," Trent maintained. He turned toward Chase, seeking confirmation. "I was trying to help. He looked weird, didn't he, Chase?"

"Yeah, you looked weird." Chase adjusted the side mirror. "You looked even weirder than usual."

"Very funny." Nathan finally recovered his balance and shifted away from Trent. "Don't hit me anymore, okay?"

"Fine, but don't look weird then," Trent said.

"Any chance that weird expression on your face had something to do with your date, Emma Montgomery?" Chase asked.

"She's not my date."

Chase nodded. "Okay. Then any chance that weird expression on your face had something to do with your not-date, Emma Montgomery?"

Nathan groaned. "No. Emma and I are just friends."

"Megan and Chase were just friends until they started having wild and wicked sex," Trent pointed out. "Maybe you and Emma are that kind of friends."

"No, we're not."

Trent grinned. "Too bad. Personally, I'm looking for

a female friend like that. Sounds like a heck of a deal to me."

"You're an idiot, Trent. No woman is ever going to want to marry you," Chase said.

Trent's grin only grew wider. "That's the general idea."

After Trent went back to admiring the car, Chase looked at Nathan. "Seriously. Are you okay?"

"Yes. Just thinking about work."

"How's the program coming along?"

"It has problems," Nathan admitted. "I'm not sure it will be ready in time for BizExpo."

"Sure it will," Trent said. "You always pull the fat out of the fire, Nathan. You will this time, too."

Nathan wished he shared his brother's confidence, but he didn't. He wasn't sure this time he could make a minor miracle happen.

But he sure hoped he could.

The back door opened, and Megan stepped out onto the porch. "Chase, honey, are you boys going to stay out here all night?"

As soon as Megan appeared, Chase's face lit up. Nathan couldn't help feeling a little jealous of the happiness his brother had found. Unlike Trent, he'd like to find someone special and build a life together in Honey.

Too bad that woman couldn't be Emma.

"We're done," Chase said, trotting over to join Megan.

"Ah, jeez," Trent said when Chase kissed his new wife. "There they go again. Hey, Chase, is this how it's going to be from now on? Whenever Megan calls, you come running?"

Chase grinned. "Oh, yeah. You bet. As fast as I can." Then he kissed his wife again, and they went inside the house.

"Face it, Trent. Chase is in love."

Trent hung his head. "It's a sad day when a man walks away from his brothers for a woman."

Nathan laughed and headed toward the house. "You really aren't ever going to find anyone to marry you, Trent."

"Amen to that," Trent said. "Amen to that."

7

Emma turned when she heard the back door open. As soon as Nathan entered the kitchen, his gaze met hers. As always, she felt a thrill of excitement dance through her.

Good grief. She didn't want to be so attracted to this man. He had roots so deep in this town they could strike oil. And his family was like one big meddlesome mob. Although she liked them, she couldn't get used to how easily they delved into each other's lives.

"Good, the men are here," Leigh said, setting the last of the dirty dinner plates on the kitchen counter. "We women are officially off duty now. Let's go sprawl in the family room, watch some sports thingy on TV, and scratch ourselves in impolite places while the guys take care of the dishes."

Emma laughed. "Um, Leigh, I'm not sure doing the dishes doesn't sound a whole lot better than what you've suggested."

"Oh, okay," Leigh said with a huff. She turned to

Azure and Megan. "I suppose you two want to do something genteel and ladylike as well."

Megan was laughing, but Azure frowned. "Why do we have to scratch?"

Leigh snorted and rolled her eyes at Trent. Then she said to Azure, "Don't worry about it, hon. Just come along."

Still muttering about not wanting to scratch anything, Azure followed Leigh, her stiletto heels clacking loudly on the wooden floor. At a little over twenty years old, Azure was the youngest person at the dinner. She also seemed the most baffled. She didn't seem to follow any of the conversations. Emma figured Azure and Trent wouldn't be dating too long. At least she hoped not, for both of their sakes.

"I'm so glad I had the chance to meet you," Megan said as she fell into step with Emma. "Leigh mentioned she was bringing a friend home from college, but with Leigh, you never know if you should anticipate something wonderful or run for cover."

Emma smiled at Megan. She really liked Chase's wife. She was smart, nice, and levelheaded. "I know what you mean about Leigh. She's something else."

"Who's something else?" Leigh asked when they reached the family room.

"You," Emma explained, settling on the overstuffed couch.

Azure frowned again. "What else are you, Leigh?"

Leigh snorted again, but Megan leaned over and patted Azure's hand. "Don't worry about it. Emma simply meant that Leigh is a bit..."

Leigh leaned forward in her chair. "Yeah, I'd like to hear this, too. I'm a bit?"

"Crazy," Emma supplied at the same time Megan said, "Wild."

Leigh laughed. "Yeah, I can be both of those things sometimes. But come on? Who can blame me? You've seen the guys I grew up with. It's a miracle I'm not in jail somewhere."

Megan and Emma both nodded.

"That's true, Leigh," Megan said. "Although I dearly love Chase, you're a model citizen compared to what you could have become after being raised by those Barrett brothers."

Azure tipped her head. "You don't like your brothers, Leigh?"

"Oh, I like them. I even love them. But they drive me up a wall sometimes."

Azure glanced around. "Which wall?"

Emma bit back a laugh, but Leigh groaned.

"It's a saying, Azure," Leigh explained.

Azure sighed. "I've never heard any of these sayings before. They must be things you old people like to say, like 'Bless my boots.'"

"Hey, I'm only a tiny bit older than you," Leigh said. "I am not old. And I have never in my life said 'Bless my boots.'"

Azure didn't seem impressed. She studied Leigh, then said, "You look so much older than me."

Leigh turned toward Emma and Megan. "Remind me to whack Trent on the head when he comes in."

Azure frowned once again. "Why?"

Deciding to step in before a war broke out, Emma

turned to Megan. "So, have you lived in Honey all of your life?"

"Most of it. How about you? You're from Austin, right?"

"That's where I live now. Growing up, my mother and I moved around the country a lot. She liked to go on what she called adventures. She'd pick a new town, and we'd move there."

"Did you enjoy moving around that much?" Megan asked.

Azure sighed loudly and stood. "I'm bored."

As she tottered out of the room on her high heels, Leigh rolled her eyes.

"Whoever said that the young are the hope for tomorrow has never met Azure," Leigh said dryly.

Emma hated to be mean, but Leigh definitely had a point.

A few seconds after Azure entered the kitchen, Nathan and Chase came into the family room.

"We thought we'd leave Trent alone with his date," Nathan said, coming to sit by Emma.

Chase sat next to Megan, who kissed him on the cheek.

"If you ask me, Trent should charge Azure's parents for babysitting," Chase said.

Megan tapped his arm. "Don't be mean."

"Hey, she called me old," he said in his defense.

"She called all of us old. She came into the kitchen and told Trent she's tired of hanging around all of us old folks and wants to go dancing."

Leigh turned to Megan and Emma. "See? This is exactly what I'm talking about. How could I possibly turn out normal with Chase, Nathan, and Trent raising me?"

"Hey," Chase said. "Trent I'll give you, but there's nothing wrong with Nathan and me."

"Oh, pulease." Leigh leaned toward Emma. "Consider yourself lucky that you're an only child."

Truthfully, Emma hadn't given much thought to not having a family before arriving in Honey. Sure, she'd been looking forward to her new job and teaching with her father. But now she was looking forward to reestablishing family in her life, to spending time with her father and getting to know him.

Of course, part of the reason she was looking forward to it was that her father was nothing like Leigh's brothers. Even though she hadn't spent much time with him, there was no way he could be like Leigh's brothers.

"You're lucky to have us," Nathan said. "Several circuses offered us good money for you, but we never once considered selling."

"Ha ha." She turned to Emma. "How do you stand working for this man? If it were me, I'd rather take out my own appendix using a rusty butter knife and salad tongs."

Emma laughed. "He's not so bad."

Nathan turned to look at her, and she found her gaze held by his. Desire washed over her. Holy cow, did this man get to her. She felt tingles straight down to her toes, and she was very glad no one in the room could read her mind.

"Thanks for the faint praise," Nathan said. Even though his words weren't seductive, the way he said them was. Emma's gaze dropped to his lips. She wanted to kiss him again. No matter how much she tried to resist him, she kept failing. Miserably.

"Hello, earth to Emma and Nathan," Leigh said.

Emma blinked and looked at her friend. Leigh had a knowing, smug expression on her face. Emma frowned. "What?"

"Not a thing," Leigh said in a singsong voice. "Not a thing. Not a single thing."

"Stop it, Leigh," Nathan said.

She grinned at him. "You love me, and you know it. Like I've said, if it weren't for me, your life would be boring."

Trent and Azure walked in at that moment.

"I'm bored, too," Azure said. "I want to go."

Leigh laughed and asked the group, "Quick, what do you call a seesaw with nothing to do?" When they all shrugged, she said, "Board."

Azure frowned. "I don't get it. Is this another of those old people sayings?"

Emma bit back a laugh and glanced at Nathan. He winked at her, and she felt her heart do a little flippy-flop.

Yep, no matter how much she tried, she was finding it impossible to resist Nathan Barrett.

🌺

NATHAN EYED THE NEWSPAPER ON TOP OF THE ROOF. Damn. How come it always ended up there? He wasn't expecting his newspaper to be resting on the doorstep when he came out each morning, but was it really too much to expect it to be on the ground? Muttering, he tossed his basketball up on the roof and watched as it bounced and rolled to the edge, thankfully knocking the paper down on its way.

"Danny, you have the worst aim of any person on this planet," he muttered as he picked up the basketball and newspaper.

"Who's Danny?" Emma asked from behind him.

He hadn't heard her walk up. "My paperboy," Nathan explained. "He always tosses my paper up on the roof."

Emma glanced at the roof and whistled. "Wow, that's quite a feat. You should have the local baseball coach put him on the team."

"I would except Danny's aiming for the porch."

She smiled. "Oh. That would be a problem." Moving up the walkway a few steps, she said, "You're awake earlier than usual."

"Couldn't sleep." Man, that was an understatement. He'd been wired when they'd gotten home from Chase's house last night, and after several restless hours, he'd finally given up and come outside to get the paper.

"What about you?" he asked.

"I get up this early every morning so I can jog before work," Emma said.

For the first time, Nathan noticed she was wearing shorts, a T-shirt, and running shoes. Her outfit was hardly racy, but it definitely got his blood pumping.

"Want to come along?" she asked with an inviting smile.

"Sure," Nathan found himself saying before his mind had a chance to override his hormones. Damn. What a stupid thing to agree to. Here he was trying his hardest to fight the attraction he felt for this woman, and he'd just agreed to jog with her.

Had he completely lost his mind?

Apparently. And since he'd agreed, Emma was smiling at him like he'd invented electricity. He certainly couldn't back out now.

"Give me a second to put on running shoes," he said. "Can't jog in jeans and cowboy boots."

She smiled. "Not hardly."

He brought the basketball and paper inside and set them in the foyer. It took him only a couple of minutes to change, and then he was back outside.

"You pick the direction," he said. "But remember, I don't jog every morning so I may have trouble keeping up with you."

"Now why don't I believe that?" She headed down the driveway at a modest pace. Nathan had no trouble keeping up with her. He worked out regularly on a treadmill. The terrain around Honey was flatter than a stagnant stock market, so jogging here was easy.

"I've never seen you out running," Nathan said when he drew near Emma.

"I always run early," she said. "Before you leave for work."

"You know what time I leave for work?"

"Sure. Seven-thirty. On the dot. Except on Saturdays. Then you go in at eight."

They headed toward town, and Nathan came to a couple of conclusions. First, he liked that Emma had paid so much attention to his schedule. And second, he realized he was the most boring man alive. He always went to work at the same time every day? He gave a rut a bad name.

"I had no idea I was so structured," he admitted, none too happy to find out that he was.

Emma glanced at him. "What's wrong with structure? It's a good thing. It gives life a framework." She smiled slightly. "I like structure. It's not something I had growing up, and now I find it comforting."

Emma found structure comforting? For a split second, Nathan felt good about that until, of course, he realized that the last thing he wanted Emma Montgomery to feel around him was comforted.

"Maybe Azure's right. Maybe I am old and boring," he said.

Emma bumped her arm against his. "Trust me you are neither old nor boring."

He grinned. "Damned by faint praise."

"Fishing for a compliment?" she teased. "I would have thought all those trophies would have fulfilled your need for praise."

Nathan chuckled. "We all need an attaboy now and then."

"Or an attagirl."

"Or an attagirl," he agreed, keeping his pace even with hers. "You've done a lot in your life to deserve praise. Was your mom the type to cheer you on?"

"Oh, yeah. Big time."

Nathan glanced at Emma. She sounded wistful, and he couldn't help wondering how long it had been since she'd had that kind of encouragement. "And your dad? Is he big on cheering for you?"

Emma smiled and shook her head. "No. He's very

proper. But he's kind and always does the right thing. That's very important, too."

"I think so."

She slowed her pace, and when Nathan shot her a questioning look, she said, "In a way, you're like him."

Nathan groaned. "I remind you of your father?"

With a laugh, Emma explained, "No. Not like that. I only meant you're kind. You think of other people. You try to do the right thing even if it isn't easy. I admire you."

"I admire you, too," he said.

"Why? For mooching a job and a place to stay from you?"

He chuckled. "No. For working hard. For throwing yourself into a project and pitching in."

This time, when Emma smiled, he could tell how pleased she was by what he'd said. But he meant it. He really admired Emma. He was all set to discuss this some more when he noticed Steve Myerson up ahead on the sidewalk tugging on Rufus' leash.

"Hey, Steve," Nathan said, wishing he and Emma hadn't been interrupted just when the conversation was getting interesting, but unable to ignore an old family friend.

"Hey, Nathan. Mind giving me a hand with Rufus? You did so well last time that I'm glad you came along. He has an appointment with the vet, but for some odd reason, I can't get him to move." Might be because Rufus hasn't moved since his last vet appointment over a year ago.

Nathan looked at the dog, then looked at Steve's minivan. Finally, he looked at Emma.

"Didn't a pink tennis ball work last time?" she asked. "Why don't you do what you did last year?"

Nathan looked at Steve, who scratched his bald head. "Don't have any of those left. The last one I cut a hole in and stuck it on the back of my van."

"What?" Emma sounded as confused as Nathan felt.

"My van doesn't have an antenna I can put it on, and I need a way to spot my van when I go to Food Factory." At their baffled expressions, he added, "That warehouse store is gargantuan, and the parking lot is huge and filled with vans, trucks, and SUVs that look like mine. I could never figure out where I'd parked. Now I just look down each aisle until I see the pink tennis ball."

Nathan doubted that anyone could miss Steve's minivan. It was purple. The older man always maintained it wasn't purple but rather deep plum.

Nathan, like the rest of Honey, simply agreed. None of them had the heart to point out to Steve that his minivan was not only purple, it was bright purple.

Putting a pink tennis ball on that van was about as necessary as tossing a lit match on the sun. There was no way anyone could ever miss Steve's minivan.

"So what do you think, Nathan?" Steve asked.

Nathan knelt next to Rufus and patted the old dog. "Feel like going for a ride?"

"Rufus doesn't much care what he does," Steve said. "Got any ideas?"

At Steve's question, Nathan turned his head—and found himself looking directly at Emma's tempting legs. Oh, yeah, he had a few ideas. None of them had a thing to do with the dog, of course. But he had ideas all right.

"Maybe I can help." Emma knelt on Rufus' other

side, and Nathan cursed losing his great view of her legs. Of course, at this angle, he now had a great view of her pretty face. She was flushed from running and looked tousled and sexy.

"Are you thinking what I'm thinking?" Emma asked.

He certainly hoped so. He smiled. She smiled back.

"Enticement. That's the key," she said softly.

Oh, yeah. That worked for him. He was one hundred percent behind the idea of enticement. He barely managed not to groan when Emma wet her lips.

"Enticement," Nathan said.

"Exactly," she said.

"Liver," Steve said.

And Nathan felt like a bucket of ice water was poured over his head. He looked over his shoulder at Steve. "Excuse me?"

"Liver. Rufus loves liver. And I've got some in the fridge. Had it for dinner last night. Hold on."

As Steve headed into the house, Nathan slowly stood.

"Liver," Emma said.

Nathan nodded. "Liver." She'd also stood, and he found himself unable to look away from her. "Was that the sort of enticement you had in mind?"

"Um, sure."

Nathan watched with fascination as a faint blush colored Emma's cheeks. He kept his gaze fixed on her face and watched her become increasingly flustered.

"I've got the liver," Steve yelled, coming back out the front door.

Emma looked at Nathan. "What else would I have meant?"

"I'd give anything to know," he said, unable to stop himself from smiling. "Anything."

A smile haunted Emma's lips, but she didn't say anything because Steve reached them with the piece of liver. Rufus barely raised his head, which for a normal dog would have been showing no interest at all. But for Rufus it was practically dancing the tango.

"See, I told you he liked liver," Steve said, giving some to the pooch.

Emma patted the dog, who remained firmly tacked to the sidewalk. "I still don't see how we're going to get him into the minivan."

"Oh, it won't be hard now that he's so excited," Steve said. He looked at Nathan. "You take the dangerous end and let the young lady here grab the safe end."

Nathan examined the dog, baffled as to which end was safe. From what he could tell, the front end drooled a lot. But the back end of a dog like Rufus was...well, frankly, unpredictable.

He looked at Emma and raised one eyebrow. She bit back a giggle.

"Come on, let's get him loaded before he realizes what you two are up to," Steve said. "I'd help, but my back hasn't been the same since the seventies." Nathan gave him a questioning look, and Steve explained with a laugh, "You know, disco."

This time, Nathan couldn't prevent himself from laughing as well. Emma laughed, too. Even Rufus seemed amused.

"Those were the days," Steve said. "Now what say we put Rufus in the minivan?"

Since there was no way to avoid the inevitable, Nathan tried to lift Rufus. Although the dog didn't seem to mind in the least, he also weighed more than a truckload of bricks.

Despite considering himself a fairly strong guy, Nathan had one heck of a time getting a grip on the dog. If he held Rufus around the waist, both ends sagged dangerously low. Emma moved forward and held up Rufus' head, so Nathan supported the back end.

"The van's over here," Steve said.

Like they could miss a huge purple minivan. "Boy, this dog weighs a ton," Emma said, huffing.

Nathan shifted his hands forward a little so he could carry more of the weight. "He's a big dog, but I think the main problem is he's so relaxed."

"If he were any more relaxed, he'd be dead," she said.

Finally, they reached the van and carefully set Rufus in the back.

Nathan looked at Steve. "Can someone help you get him out at the vet's? You won't be able to do it alone, especially not with your back problems."

"Oh, don't worry about that. Doc Williams comes out to the car to give Rufus his yearly shots. Seems easier." He again scratched his shiny head. "But I will need some help when I get home. Don't suppose you could stop by this afternoon?"

Emma looked horrified by the idea, so Nathan said, "We'll be at work. But I'll make sure Trent and Leigh stop by to give you a hand."

Steve grinned. "Thanks. I appreciate it."

After the older man climbed in his van and drove off, Nathan looked at Emma.

"I smell like lazy dog," he said.

With a strangled sound, she sat on the curb, her hands covering her face. Concerned, Nathan sat next to her. "Are you crying?"

When she lifted her head, he saw she was laughing. "No. I've never worked so hard in my life not to smile."

"Yeah, Rufus is something else."

"I can't remember ever having so much fun." She laughed again. "The dangerous end? Which end is that?"

Nathan grinned. "It was a toss-up, I'll tell you. I wasn't sure what to do for a minute there."

"This town is unique; I'll give you that."

He liked to think so. "Yeah, Honey's a fun place. Sort of the entertainment capital of the middle of nowhere."

She grinned back at him. "I don't know about you, but I really need a shower. Badly. I also smell like lazy dog."

Nathan stood and helped her up. "Come on. Let's go become human again."

Rather than jog, they walked on the return trip, laughing repeatedly about Rufus. When they finally got back to his house, Emma waved, then dashed upstairs to her apartment to clean up.

Nathan headed inside his house, wondering at what point he'd become so attracted to Emma that even covered with dog fur and smelling like Rufus, she was the most compelling woman he'd ever met.

8

"Hi...um, Dad," Emma said two weeks later when she called her father. As always, she stumbled when calling him Dad. Prior to recently, she'd only spoken to her father a few times a year. Now she called him a couple of times a month, but even with the extra communication, their conversations were often stilted. She only hoped that would change once she moved to Wyneheart.

"Emma, dear, how are you? How is that job in Hummus working out?" As always, her father sounded distracted. She could hear papers rustling in the background. No doubt he was working while at the same time talking to her.

She had a perfect image of him in her mind from her last visit to Wyneheart. He probably was sitting behind his huge desk, his papers systematically organized, a clock prominently displayed so he kept on schedule at all times. Unlike her own desk, on Benjamin Montgomery's desk, there were no papers slipping off the sides like lemmings plunging into the sea, no reference books teetering in Leaning Tower of Pisa piles, no half-consumed rolls of antacids scattered around.

No, Benjamin Montgomery's desk was neat, organized, and efficient. Emma couldn't help wondering what he was going to think once she finally moved to Massachusetts, and he saw how disorganized she could be at times.

He would probably have an embolism.

"Honey. The job is in Honey, Dad, not Hummus."

"Ah, so it is. Sorry, dear. Anyway, how is Honey? I'm sure the place is dreadful."

"Honey is great. I've met a lot of very friendly people here. And Barrett Software is a terrific place to work. Very advanced."

"If it's so advanced, why don't they locate their headquarters where the industry is growing? Someplace like Silicon Valley or on the East Coast."

"Because the owner, Nathan Barrett, is very loyal to Honey. He was born here and knows the town depends on him."

"Hmm," was all her father said, so she knew he wasn't listening to her again. The workings of small-town Honey didn't interest him.

"So how are you?" she asked.

"Wonderful. Busy. Yesterday, I was struck by a brilliant idea for a new book, examining symbolism in Whitman. Not the same old, same old. Instead, it will take a new approach. I've already roughed out the outline and can't wait to start writing. And how are you?"

How was she? She wasn't sure what to say to that.

She was...confused. Confused by the feelings she had for Nathan. Confused as to what would happen to her if she acted on those feelings. Over the past couple of weeks, she and Nathan had both worked hard at being friends. But the memory of the kisses they'd shared danced between them like an annoying ghost. Whenever she was in the room with Nathan, she became confused about so many things.

Like how was she going to feel ten years from now if she didn't act on the feelings she had for him? And she had deep feelings for the man. She admired him. She wanted him. She liked him. And he confused her.

But her father wasn't the person to discuss those feelings with. He was trying. He really was. But he didn't have a clue how to be a father, and he certainly didn't know what to do with a female offspring. If she poured her heart out to her dad, she'd end up embarrassing both of them.

Instead, she settled for the simple answer. "I'm fine."

"And your dissertation? Are you almost done?"

Um, if one considered almost done to be roughly a third of the way through it.

"Not quite," she admitted, feeling ridiculously like an errant child.

"Emma, goals don't achieve themselves," her father said. "You must pursue them relentlessly. Victory belongs to those who claim it. A winner is the one who never relaxes. Always keep your eye on the horizon, your focus on the achievement, and your hand on the helm."

Oh, great. Just what she needed. Cross-stitch adages. "I know, Dad."

"Seriously, what seems to be the problem? You should be done by now."

Emma couldn't tell him the problem was Nathan. The man got to her. Every time she was near him, she felt as if she'd just gotten off a Loop-D-Loop ride at a carnival. He confused her to the point that whenever she sat down to work on her dissertation, she ended up thinking about him instead.

She'd called her father hoping to refocus her energies. Now that she thought about it, his sayings were exactly what she needed. She should write them down and slap them on the wall next to her desk. She needed to pursue her dreams like a fox hot on a rabbit's tail. She needed to keep her eye on the goal and her hand on the...no, wait, had it been her hand on the goal and her eye on the helm? She frowned. That didn't sound right. Well, whatever he'd said, she agreed with it. She needed to keep her hormones under lock and key and her lips to herself.

Maybe that's what she needed to put on the wall next to her computer.

"I'm making progress," she told her father. "And I'm going to make even more over the next couple of weeks."

"That's my girl," her father said, and unexpected warmth flowed through Emma. Yes, she was his girl. Even though they didn't know each other very well, they were both working hard to make up for the past. She wasn't alone in this world. She had family.

Okay, maybe not family in the way Nathan had family, but she wasn't sure she could take having a family like his. The Barretts had good intentions, but they were a crazy bunch.

She'd take her organized, practical father any day. Together, they formed a sane, rational family.

❧

"READY FOR SOME GOOD NEWS?"

Nathan glanced up as Emma entered his office carrying a stack of papers. During the past few weeks, she'd worked long hours helping Barrett Software flatten the problems with Simplify. She'd done whatever anyone asked—pitched in on the testing, run reports, and even wrote some of the online helps. She was a smart, dedicated lady.

"I love good news." Nathan stood and crossed the room to take the papers from her. He hadn't meant to touch her, but his hands brushed hers when he took the report. They both felt the contact, and for a minute, simply stared at each other. Then Emma took a step back from him.

"Those are the results from the latest batch of tests. Tim dropped the report off on his way home," she said with a slightly breathless hitch to her voice.

Nathan forced himself to ignore the attraction he felt to Emma and studied the papers instead. When he read the information, he let out a hoot. "Hot damn. The latest tests went great. Almost every function works flawlessly."

Emma grinned. "I know. Congratulations."

"Congratulations to all of us. You included. You've really been a big help."

He could tell she was pleased by his compliment. A light flush colored her pretty face. "Thanks for saying that."

"I mean it." And he did. He really appreciated all the help she'd given the team. He also appreciated the help she'd given him. She'd helped keep him on schedule. But more than that, he liked having her around. Being with Emma made him happy.

"I'm having fun," she said softly, her gaze locking with his. "I'm glad I came to work here."

"I'm glad you're here, too." He found himself taking a step closer to her. Desire slammed into him like a fist.

Don't kiss her, you idiot.

Emma tipped her head slightly. Her gaze moved from his eyes to his lips. He could easily tell she was thinking what he was thinking.

Do not kiss her!

Nathan struggled to remember all the reasons why he shouldn't kiss Emma. He knew there were reasons. Lots of them. Too bad he couldn't think of a single one at the moment, and since he couldn't, he did the next best thing.

He smiled at her and asked, "May I kiss you?"

She smiled back and nodded, then moved forward at the same moment he did.

He knew this was a mistake, but he didn't care. He kissed her.

***

AS ALWAYS, NATHAN'S KISS MADE EMMA WILD WITH desire. But now, there was more. Much more. Kissing

Nathan felt right. Felt perfect. She felt as if she'd finally found where she belonged.

So she kept on kissing him, and kissing him, and kissing him until the sound of the elevator in the distance made them both realize where they were and what they were doing.

"The cleaning crew," Nathan said when they stopped kissing and reluctantly stepped apart.

"Yes," was all Emma could think to say.

"Guess we should head home," he said.

"Yes."

Nathan smiled slowly. "Are you going to agree to whatever I suggest?"

Emma knew he was teasing her, but she wasn't when she answered, "Yes."

Nathan looked at her. Emma felt her heart beating like a hummingbird's wings as she waited for his reaction.

Please don't say no.

Finally, he asked, "Does that yes mean—"

"It means yes." She gave him a slow, seductive smile, and she watched understanding dawn on him. "The next move is up to you, hotshot. You know where to find me."

With that, she headed out of his office, stopping by her desk on the way to get her purse. At the elevator, she ended up having to wait for the cleaning crew to exit, then she got in and took it to the lobby. As she walked across the parking lot, she kept hoping against hope that she'd hear Nathan running to catch up with her.

But the night remained silent except for the sound

of distant traffic. Oh well. He'd no doubt leave in a few minutes and meet her back at the house. He probably wanted to think this over. She only hoped he came to the right conclusion.

Leigh maintained Nathan was never wrong. Well, Emma hoped he didn't make the wrong decision this time. The right decision was to become her lover. She was tired of playing this game of cat and mouse. He wanted her. She wanted him. They should be together.

As she drove to Nathan's house, she kept checking her rearview mirror, looking for signs that he might be following her. But he wasn't. No headlights appeared behind her, and she couldn't help being disappointed. Had she really misread Nathan? It didn't seem possible. The man had just kissed her silly.

But he hadn't followed her home. So after parking her car, she headed up the steps to her apartment, cursing men in general and Nathan Barrett in particular. How could he not want her, too? She knew he wanted her. She was positive he wanted her.

"Darn him," she muttered, unlocking her door.

"Darn who?"

Emma squeaked and spun around. Nathan stood at the bottom of the steps.

"I thought you weren't interested," she said breathlessly, thrilled to see him.

He chuckled and bounded up the stairs. "You can't be serious. Me? Not be interested? Not possible."

"But I didn't hear you leave your office. And you didn't follow me home," she said, glancing around, looking for his car. "Hey, I didn't hear you pull up, either."

Nathan reached the top of the stairs and slipped his arms around her waist, tugging her close. "That's because I got here ahead of you."

"How? I left before you."

Nathan's grin was pure devil. "No, you didn't. The second you walked out, I sprinted down the stairs. No way was I going to give you a chance to change your mind." He reached over her shoulder and pushed open the door to her apartment.

Emma laughed as he backed her through the doorway, his arms never moving from around her waist.

"You're sure about this, right?" he asked after they were inside, and he'd shut the door.

"Yes." She leaned up and kissed him deeply. "I'm very, very sure. We both know this isn't about being together for a lifetime. But why should we waste what time we do have?"

"I like the way you think, Ms. Montgomery."

She laughed. "Why, thank you, Mr. Barrett. I'm pleased you agree with me."

9

Emma was lost in thought when she entered Nathan's office and went to place some papers on his desk. She'd hardly seen him since they'd become lovers. Simplify was keeping everyone running. But they were making progress at last, and Emma knew that if anyone could pull this off, it would be Nathan. The man was amazing.

And she missed being with him. Their lovemaking had been wonderful, truly wonderful. As she'd expected, he was a tender, thoughtful, exciting lover.

She started to set the papers down, then froze when she saw what was on his desk.

"I don't believe it," she muttered. Caitlin Estes had sent a full sheet cake to Nathan with her picture on it. And not just any old picture. In the shot, she was in her cheerleading uniform. Again. Good grief. Apparently, Caitlin had had a lot of success in that uniform because she obviously thought it would do the trick with Nathan.

A not-so-tiny part of Emma took satisfaction in the knowledge that Nathan was no longer available. At least, he wasn't at the moment. At the moment, he was hers. All hers.

Of course, he was just a loaner. She had no ownership rights where Nathan was concerned. All too soon, she'd be gone from Honey. Then maybe Caitlin would succeed in her plan to catch his attention.

Emma sighed. Drat. She hated that thought. She hated the thought of Nathan with anyone but her. But the reality of her relationship with Nathan was that he had to stay here. And she had to leave. She had a job waiting for her in Massachusetts.

As simple as that. She pulled her roll of antacids out of her pocket. Boy, life really stunk sometimes.

"Are you nervous about Simplify?" Nathan asked, walking up to stand next to her and nodding at the antacids in her hand.

Emma grabbed the excuse he offered. "Yes. Do you think it will be ready in time for the show?"

"Yes." He took the roll of antacids from her, then shut his office door. "You don't seem to get as nervous as you used to. I rarely see you using these things anymore. Any reason why you need them today?"

Emma took the antacids from him and slipped them back into her pocket. "I've been more relaxed this summer, but today, I've been thinking about my dissertation a lot."

He grinned. "So you're relaxed this summer? I wonder why?"

She had to laugh at that. "I'm going back to work.

The boss is a real dragon, and I don't want him yelling at me."

Nathan continued to grin at her. "Fine. Run away. See if I care."

"Oh, you care all right. I know you do." She nodded toward his desk. "By the way, Caitlin struck again."

Nathan walked over to his desk and studied the cake. "Will this woman ever get the idea that I'm not interested in her?"

"You have to give her points for perseverance," Emma said. "She knows what she wants and isn't going to give up."

"It's not going to do her any good. Sometimes you have to accept reality. If something isn't going to work, it isn't going to work."

Emma nodded. Yep. He was right. Sometimes you had to accept reality, even if it stunk.

"I'm going back to work," she said, heading for the door before she did something foolish like kiss him. Or cry. She definitely didn't want to cry.

"Emma."

She turned and looked at him. "Yes?"

"I'm sorry I've been stuck at work so much. I'd like to spend time with you."

She nodded again. She definitely wanted to spend time with him as well. Feeling a tightening in her throat, she quickly headed out the door. Blast it all. She wasn't going to cry. She absolutely wasn't. She rarely cried, and she certainly wasn't going to today.

And she wasn't going to do anything really stupid like fall for Nathan. She was way too smart for that. The last thing she wanted to take with her when she left Honey was a broken heart.

❧

NATHAN HAD JUST GOTTEN HOME FROM WORK WHEN he bumped into Leigh in the foyer. She was sitting on a suitcase, obviously waiting for him. "What's up?"

"I'm going to stay with Trent," she said.

That didn't make any sense. Leigh and Trent were too much alike to get along. Their fights were the stuff of local legend. "Why?"

She shrugged. "I want to spend some time with him."

"But he lives in Honey. You see him all the time. More than once a day at least."

Leigh looked Nathan dead in the eye. "I'm going, which means that your house will be empty. You will be the only person here, so it's not like anyone will know anything that happens in this house while no one is here."

Nathan chuckled. "I have no idea what you just said."

"Jeez, you're dense. Nathan, think. You will be alone in the house," she said slowly.

Nathan knew what she was telling him. He and Emma would be without their chaperone. He just hadn't realized that Leigh knew the two of them wanted to be alone. He also hadn't realized Leigh knew why they wanted to be alone.

Then again, he wasn't sure why he was surprised. Everyone in this town always knew everything. Probably people at the grocery store were talking about his relationship with Emma.

"This is unnecessary," he said. "You don't have to leave. I'm spending almost all of my time at the office. In fact, I'm heading back tonight. You can stay here."

Leigh snorted. "You won't always be at the office. And I don't want you to have to sneak into your own house from that garage at four in the morning every day. You're really bad at it and make way too much noise."

"How did you know I—" He skittered to a verbal stop when a new and scary thought occurred to him. "Why were you awake at four in the morning?"

She frowned. "Hey, I'm actively not interfering in your life. The least you can do is actively not interfere in mine."

She had a point, so Nathan nodded. "Okay. Consider the question withdrawn."

Leigh made a big production out of grabbing her suitcase. "Good. Now I've got to run. Trent doesn't know I'm coming. I want to scare him."

"Leigh, you can't simply barge in on Trent. Maybe he has a reason he'd like to be alone in his house, too."

She laughed. "Trent and Azure broke up right after the dinner at Chase's house. You need to keep up with what's going on around you, Nathan. Jeez, you'd think you were focusing on your own life or something."

"You don't have to do this," he said one last time.

She winked. "Yes, I do. And seriously, have fun. But don't break Emma's heart."

"I would never do that," he said.

"Yeah, yeah, that's what all guys say. Right up until the moment when they break our hearts."

With that, she headed out the front door. A couple of minutes later, there was a knock on the back door. Nathan wasn't a bit surprised to find Emma standing there.

She looked confused. "Leigh just stopped by and said you wanted to see me."

Nathan came over and slipped his arms around her waist. "Leigh has decided to go stay with Trent for a while. Apparently, she thinks there's some reason why I need my privacy."

Emma fluttered her eyelashes. "Gee, Mr. Barrett, I can't imagine what reason that would be."

He feathered kisses on her face. "I don't know, Ms. Montgomery. Do you think if the two of us think really hard, we can come up with a reason?"

"Um, I'm pretty sure we can think of one or two."

Nathan laughed. "Then why don't we go upstairs and—"

"Wait."

Nathan blinked. "And wait?"

"No," she said with a laugh. "Well, yes. I mean you need to wait here."

With that, she pulled free of his arms and dashed out the back door.

"Guess I must have lost my touch," Nathan muttered. He knew he shouldn't be fooling around with Emma. What he should be doing was changing his clothes and heading back into the office. But he couldn't bring himself to do it tonight. Not when he had the chance to be with Emma.

Before he had time to get lonely, Emma was back. In her hand, she had a box, which she tossed to him.

"Here you go, hotshot. I bought these today." Nathan looked at the box, then back at Emma. "You bought neon-colored condoms?"

"I figured we could have a lot of fun if we had a whole box of colors to choose from."

Nathan laughed and hugged her again. "You're crazy."

"Maybe," she said with a sexy smile. "But I'm positive my theory is correct. So let's go test it out, okay?"

"Sounds like a great idea."

❧

EMMA RUBBED THE TENSION FROM HER NECK AND tried to refocus on the computer in front of her. Boy, she was tired. Really, really tired. For the past week, she and Nathan had practically lived at the office. She'd even started missing her morning jogs so she could come to work early with him.

And when they were home, well, they weren't getting a lot of sleep. She was way too aware of how few hours she had left with Nathan to waste many of them sleeping.

All of which meant she was tired but very, very happy.

"I think we may pull this off after all," Nathan said, walking into her small office.

She smiled at him. "Really?"

"Yes. The testing group said they've pounded on the remaining code and haven't found any more problems. And trust me, those people are relentless. If the code was going to break, they'd make it happen."

"Nathan, that's wonderful." As much as she wanted to walk over and kiss him, she wouldn't at work. She had made a point of keeping their personal relationship out of the office when other people were around. Still, she was tempted.

"What's wonderful?" Leigh asked, wandering in. She flopped into the chair across the desk from Emma and glanced from her brother to Emma. "Are you two keeping secrets from me?" She laughed. "Oh, right, I forgot. This is Honey. No one has any secrets."

"Unfortunately, you're right. So if you must know, I was telling Emma that it looks like Simplify is ready to go."

"Wow, not a moment too soon," Leigh pointed out.

"Yes, so now you can understand why I think it's wonderful that the program works," Emma said to her friend.

Leigh looked at Emma, a questioning expression on her face. "I can understand why this is great. But I kind of thought there were some other wonderful things going on in your life right now, too. I'm interested in those things as well."

Emma felt the warmth of a blush color her cheeks, but she refused to be embarrassed. "This is Honey, the land of no secrets."

Leigh laughed and looked from Emma to Nathan then back to Emma. "So now that things with the program have worked out, you two think there's any chance other things will work out?"

Emma found her gaze drifting to Nathan. "Things will turn out the way they're supposed to turn out."

Nathan gave her a small, resigned smile. "True."

Leigh groaned. "Great. Just great. You two are going to give up without a fight. I cannot believe this."

Turning his attention to his sister, Nathan asked, "And how are things with Jared? Did they work out?"

"Real cute, Nathan. You know the rodeo people have all left. But just because things didn't work out for me doesn't mean they can't work out for the two of you."

"Why do you care, Leigh?" Nathan asked.

"Because I like you guys. I want to see you happy. You're really disappointing me."

Nathan looked at Emma. "She's disappointed because she likes that I'm too busy with my own life to butt into hers."

Leigh pressed one hand against her chest. "*Moi*? Have ulterior motives? Not possible."

Both Nathan and Emma laughed.

"It's true," Leigh protested but without a lot of conviction.

"I'm pretty sure you've had ulterior motives from the day you were born," Nathan said.

Leigh shrugged, a smile on her face. "Could be. But you know, this time, I'm right. You two should consider putting up a little more fight, you know. Things don't always have to turn out the way things are meant to, you know. Sometimes, you can force them to go your way. Like that old fax machine. Give it a good whack, and it will work."

Emma wished Leigh were right. But what her friend wasn't taking into consideration was all that either she or Nathan would have to give up in order to be together. Nathan would have to walk away from the town he loved and the people who depended on him.

And she would miss out on the chance to finally get to connect with her father. Not only that, but she would also lose a job that was perfect for her, one she'd spent years working toward.

Those weren't exactly easy things to overcome.

When Emma glanced at Nathan, he was watching her. No doubt he was thinking the same thing she was. If there were a way, they both would probably find it. Because they cared about each other. A lot.

But was this love? And if it was, would it last? Was what they felt worth giving up everything for?

Tough, tough questions.

Leigh slapped her hands against the arms of her chair. "Well, I can tell you two have absolutely nothing to say to me, so I'm going to leave now. I haven't bothered Trent in at least four hours, so it's about time I go drive him crazy."

She grinned at Nathan and Emma. "You two have fun now. And remember what I said. There are always options if you just know how to hunt them down. Don't give up without a fight."

❧

NATHAN GLANCED OVER AT EMMA. HE WAS GLAD HE'D talked her into riding with him to Dallas for the computer show. Over the past couple of days, he'd thought about what Leigh had said. Although he rarely took his sister's advice, for obvious reasons, he couldn't help thinking she was right this time. Maybe he and

Emma should try a little harder to make their relationship work.

For starters, there were a lot of things they needed to discuss, and they were running out of time. This drive was the perfect opportunity.

"Hi," she said, waking up from a nap. She gave him a sweet, sleepy smile, and he wrapped his hands tighter around the steering wheel.

Tell her, you coward.

"Did you say something?" she asked.

He certainly hoped not. He cleared his throat. "No. But there is something I want to tell you."

"What? Is it about the program?"

"No." He refocused his attention on the road, trying to decide whether this was a smart move or emotional suicide. Maybe he should just leave things as they were. He didn't have to tell Emma how he felt. He could just leave it alone.

But he'd hate himself if he did that.

He glanced at her again. She raised one eyebrow. "Is this some big secret or something? What, are you really an alien from another planet and now that we've made love, I may give birth to a part human, part squid child?"

He laughed. "Uh, no. That wasn't what I was going to say."

She grinned. "Good, because there is no way I'm changing the diapers on a half-squid baby."

Leave it to Emma to make him laugh. He looked back at the road. He'd never told a woman he was in love with her before and frankly wasn't sure what was the right approach.

"Yes? Nathan, you're killing me with the suspense. At least tell me if this is a good thing or a bad thing."

"A good thing. At least, I think so."

A semi-truck was passing him, so he waited until it went by before continuing.

She reached over and patted his leg. "Then tell me. This isn't like you to act so shy."

That got him. "I'm not being shy."

"Okay, then coy."

"Hey, I'm a guy. I'm never coy," he maintained.

"Oops. Sorry. Didn't mean to offend you. So okay, what is it? Just blurt it out in a manly fashion."

He frowned. "Emma, I'm in...what I mean is that I'm..."

Man, why was this so difficult to say?

"Nathan, what in the world are you trying to say?"

He drew in a deep breath, then went for broke.

"I love you."

He wasn't sure what response he expected from her, but it sure wasn't the absolute silence that greeted him. Complete, absolute silence.

Way to go, Barrett. Now she'll probably never talk to you again. Guaranteed way to send the lady running for the hills.

"I'm not expecting anything of you, Emma," he assured her. "I know you have plans, and I know you can't stay in Honey. I just wanted to let you know how I feel about you."

He heard her draw in a shaky breath. "I'm not sure what to say," she admitted.

Although he hadn't expected her to say she also loved him, it still smarted when she didn't reciprocate his feelings.

He cleared his throat. "I just wanted you to know. You don't need to say anything."

And she didn't. Say anything. She didn't say she loved him. She didn't say she liked him. Heck, at this point, he would have settled for a "Can't we just be friends?" remark.

But Emma took him at his word.

She didn't say a thing. Not one damn thing.

Not a good sign at all.

🐚

"CAN YOU BELIEVE THIS CROWD?" TIM SAID TO EMMA as they stood at the Barrett Software booth watching Nathan do yet another demo of Simplify.

"It's amazing. He's already been interviewed by a couple of newspapers and three magazines," Emma said, thrilled the product was doing so well. "The voice control component is a big hit."

"This will make Barrett Software huge," Tim said.

Emma agreed. The booth had been constantly surrounded over the past two days, and even now, Nathan was still running a demo of the product to a large group of interested buyers. She was thrilled for him and for everyone else at Barrett Software.

She grabbed a stack of the info cards and along with Tim, handed them out to the crowd. Once she was done, she indulged herself and watched Nathan for a few minutes. She had to admit, he was a charmer. Everyone loved him.

Of course, it helped that Simplify worked flawlessly. But in a swamped place like this, the attendees had a couple of hundred different displays they could go to, but huge groups stopped at their booth because Nathan pulled them in. She couldn't help noticing that a lot of the visitors to their booth were female. Not that she could blame them. He was smart. He was witty. He was handsome. He was wonderful. And...

And she loved him. The realization hit her like a tidal wave. Wow. As she stood there, watching him, Emma drew in a shaky breath. She really was in love with Nathan. Hopelessly, stupidly, blindly in love with a man who was all wrong for her.

Why hadn't she done something easy, like fall for a guy who lived on Mars? Because when it came right down to it, Honey was almost as far away from the life she planned on building in Massachusetts.

How had she let this happen? What was she going to do now?

"This is going great," Nathan said after he finished the presentation.

Emma nodded. "Yes. Great."

He leaned closer and inspected her face. "I know I ask this a lot, but are you okay?"

With effort, Emma forced herself to smile. "Yes. I'm fine."

"Are you tired?"

"A little." She kept staring at him, stunned by her own feelings. She loved him. Really, truly, deeply loved him. The emotion was so intense and startling that she almost blurted it out to him in the middle of the demo booth.

Good grief.

Nathan glanced around. "Tim and the others can

handle the crowds for a while. Why don't we take a break? I'll buy you a soda."

She hesitated. Was being alone with Nathan right now a good idea?

He leaned closer and murmured, "I'll flirt with you."

Unable to stop herself, she smiled. "Oh, okay."

As Emma followed him to the small cafe and got a soda, she debated whether she should tell him how she felt. But the more she thought about not telling him, the more she mentally kicked herself for being a wimp. Nathan had been honest with her. She needed to be honest in return.

Drat!

But was being a coward really such a bad thing? Lots of famous people had been cowards. Plus, what good would come from him knowing? In fact, he might think that since they both loved each other that she was willing to give up her dreams to stay with him, which wouldn't happen. So why tell him?

"Do you want to sit in here or outside?" Nathan asked.

She sighed. She couldn't chicken out, no matter how tempting the idea might be. The man deserved to know he was loved in return.

But why did it seem as if doing the right thing was never easy? You'd think just once in a while, life would give you a break. But she wasn't getting one today, that was for sure.

She glanced around the cramped room. "Let's go outside."

"It's hot out there," he said.

Emma figured they wouldn't be out there long. How

much time did it take to tell someone you loved them but wanted to stop seeing them? Five minutes? Ten?

Ought to go pretty quickly.

"Okay." Nathan carried the sodas and waited for Emma to precede him. When she walked outside, a blast of hot air hit her. Figured. She literally would be in a hot seat this afternoon.

Heading to the table in the farthest corner, Emma sat and took her soda from Nathan.

Nathan glanced around, then teased, "If you'd picked a table any farther away, we'd be back home in Honey."

Nodding, Emma fumbled in her pocket and pulled out an antacid.

"Oh, no. Something's wrong," Nathan said, his attitude now serious. "What happened?"

Emma chewed the chalky tablet and debated how to word this conversation. She needed to phrase her confession delicately. She needed to draw on her skills as an English major to handle this well. "Nathan, we need to talk."

"That doesn't sound good. Not good at all. Can I have one of those antacids?" he asked.

Emma smiled. "I think you'll be fine."

"I'm not so sure. You look pretty serious." He took a sip of his soda, then said, "Okay. I'm set. What's wrong?"

"You're not facing a firing squad."

"Feels that way," he said, his gaze locked with hers.

Yes, it did. Especially since as much as she loved Nathan, after she told him about her feelings, she also planned to tell him what he didn't want to hear. She had to tell him that as soon as they got back to Honey, she planned on packing and returning to Austin.

Love or no love, they didn't have a future together, and it would be better in the long run if they stopped seeing each other right now. She needed to end this quickly, efficiently. Her heart was going to break, sure. But she needed to put Nathan and Honey, Texas, behind her if she was ever going to get on with her life.

Of course, she didn't need a crystal ball to know Nathan wasn't going to like that she was leaving. But he had to know. She couldn't let him think they were going to live happily ever after.

She cleared her throat. He sat watching her closely. "Um, Nathan, do you remember how on the drive here you told me you love me?"

He pretended to consider her question, but there was a definite twinkle in his eyes. "Let me think. We talked about the weather. We talked about BizExpo and Simplify. But love? Did we discuss love? Let me think for a second."

She sighed and drummed her fingers on the table. "You know very well what you told me on the drive. You said you loved me."

He gave her a gentle smile, but she could tell he was expecting more from this conversation than she was going to deliver. "Okay, yes. I remember I told you I love you. I also remember you didn't say anything back. Not one single word."

"Well, I'm saying something now. Nathan Barrett, I love you, too."

❧ 10 ❧

Anxiously, Emma waited for his reaction. Thankfully, he grinned and indicated the nearby crowd.

"You picked a heck of a time to tell me," he said. "But I'm very happy to hear you feel that way. I think the first thing we should do is—"

"No."

He raised one eyebrow. "No?"

"That's right. No."

Before he could misunderstand, Emma added, "We can't have a life together. And even though I love you, I believe we should stop seeing each other."

She'd obviously stunned him. He leaned forward and said, "That wasn't exactly what I had in mind."

"I know. But just because we love each other doesn't mean we're meant to be together. We want different things. Have different plans."

Nathan leaned back in his chair. "You have to give

me a minute here. The woman I love just told me she loves me, too. I need to enjoy that for a while."

Emma sighed. "Nathan, I think we should—"

He held up one hand. "Wait. I'm not through enjoying it yet."

Despite the seriousness of the topic, Emma laughed. "You nut."

He grinned. "Emma, I know what you're going to say, but I still can't help being thrilled that you love me, too. Even if we both want different things out of life. And even if we can never make this work, I'm blown away that you love me."

Before she could answer, he stood and circled to her side of the table. Then he kissed her, long and deep. "I've never been in love before. It's an amazing feeling."

"Yes, it is." Emma patted the side of his face. "And you're an amazing man. But—"

Nathan chuckled and leaned away from her. "Nope. No buts. Not yet. Let's enjoy the being in love part for a while."

"But after we get home, I need to pack up and head to Austin," she said. "It doesn't matter that we love each other."

Nathan walked over and sat back down. "Oh, yes, it does. It matters very much."

"You know what I mean. What difference does it make if we love each other? We can't make this relationship work."

For the longest time, Nathan simply looked at her. Happiness practically radiated off him. Finally, he said, "I know we can't last forever. But we love each other. That has to count for something."

She'd expected this discussion to be difficult. She just hadn't planned on impossible. "We both want different things out of life."

"Couldn't we change what we want? I vote that we develop new plans," he said. "I vote that we don't throw away what we feel for each other."

Emma twisted her hands in her lap, wondering what was the best way to make him understand.

"Nathan, although I love you, I can't tear my life apart. For all either one of us knows, this love we feel won't even last. It could be simply really strong lust."

"It will last," he said firmly. "It isn't just lust."

"You don't know that."

"Yes, I do. You need to have faith in us."

She sighed and fought back the urge to cry. Crying wouldn't help anything. Instead, she tried to formulate another approach.

"Okay, let's say we decide to be together. Which one of us gives up everything? Do you leave Barrett Software? And if you do, what happens to Honey? Or do I miss out on the chance to finally get to know my father, something both he and I have been looking forward to for a long, long time? So which should it be, Nathan? You hurt the people of Honey or I hurt my father?"

"Emma, there's got to be a way," he muttered.

"I don't know what it would be."

He looked determined. "I'll think of something. Solving problems is one of my best talents. I'll solve this one, too."

She wanted to believe him. Oh boy, she wanted to believe him. But she sure didn't see how to make this work. Still, she couldn't help holding on to the glimmer of hope he offered.

"I guess we'd better get back to the booth," she said, standing.

Nathan stood as well. "I will solve this," he said. She doubted it. But she gave him a small smile. Then together, they headed back to the booth in silence, each of them lost in their own thoughts, but both of them wishing life could be different.

❦

EMMA GATHERED THE LAST OF HER CLOTHES AND struggled to fit them into her one remaining suitcase. Why was it that clothes that came out of a suitcase never seemed to fit back in it right? She hadn't bought anything while in Honey. No I Survived Honey T-shirts. No cowboy clothes at the rodeo. So why wouldn't the stupid things fit?

After repeated attempts, she resorted to banging on the suitcase. She wasn't in the mood to fight with her clothes right now. She just wanted to go back to Austin and start working on fixing her broken heart.

She was banging so hard on the suitcase that it took her a minute to realize someone was knocking on her door. She fought back the thrill of excitement she felt. It wouldn't be Nathan. He had avoided her as much as she'd avoided him since they'd gotten back from Dallas yesterday.

When she opened her door, Leigh stood outside. "Hi."

"Hi."

Leigh frowned. "You look like hell."

Emma imagined she did. "I've been packing to go back to Austin."

"I thought you weren't leaving for another three days?"

Emma shrugged. "I decided there was nothing left for me to do here, so I might as well head on home."

With a snort, Leigh said, "No offense, but you're a terrible liar."

"What? I'm not lying. I'm—"

Cutting Emma off, Leigh continued, "You're lying to me, and you're lying to yourself. You love Nathan, and you know it. Everyone in town knows it."

"We don't love each other," Emma said, but rather than a stern protest, the words came out as almost a sigh.

Leigh snorted again. "Don't throw away happiness, Emma."

"Leigh, even if we did love each other, it could never work. I have to think of my father. He and I have plans."

"Have you asked him what he thinks you should do?"

"No," Emma admitted.

"You should," Leigh said. Then she turned and headed down the stairs. "Talk to you later. I just thought of something I need to do. But before you leave, Emma, call your father. Tell him what's happening."

Emma stood at the top of the stairs to her apartment, staring after Leigh. Her friend was wrong. Dead wrong. Asking her father what he thought was unfair.

She'd made promises to him. Promises she couldn't break.

Shutting the door, Emma glared at her suitcase.

Shirts and jeans hung out the sides like the arms of an octopus. Maybe she could find a box or a bag around here and put some of the clothes into it. She went over to the closet and poked around, finally finding an old box in the back. After snagging the box, she was all set to toss her errant clothes inside when she realized the box wasn't empty. It contained several framed pictures.

Despite herself, Emma sat on the sofa and took out a few of the pictures. They were of Nathan and his brothers and sister. In each shot, the four of them were clowning and joking and laughing. The Barrett siblings might fuss, but they really loved each other a lot.

"They're so lucky." She rooted through the box and brought out the remaining two pictures. One was a school portrait of Leigh. Emma figured her friend was in first or second grade in the picture. She had a big green and blue bow on the top of her head and looked ready to kill the photographer.

Emma laughed, then looked at the last picture. It was of Nathan at approximately the same age. He was missing his two front teeth, but that didn't stop him from flashing a killer smile at the photographer.

Always the charmer. Even in grade school.

Emma traced her thumb across his face and felt the warmth of tears on her cheeks. Drat. She'd promised herself she wouldn't cry. Crying was silly and useless. She'd made the right decision. She had. Leaving was the right thing to do.

"Stop it right now," she said. "I mean it. Stop crying

right now, or I won't buy any fudge ripple ice cream for a month."

Despite her threat, the tears kept falling.

"This is ridiculous," she said, sniffling. She headed toward the kitchen and grabbed a tissue. Blotting the tears didn't seem to help, either. Nothing seemed to help.

Without thinking, she grabbed the phone and dialed. Her father answered on the first ring.

"Emma, dear, it's so good to hear from you. I was talking to Marge Adler today. She teaches American Literature and like the rest of the English Department, can't wait for you to arrive."

Emma sniffled. Oh terrific. More waterworks. "That's great," she said, hoping her overly cheerful voice would cover up the sounds of her crying.

A long, long, long silence greeted her. Finally, her father asked, "Emma, are you crying?"

The way he said the word crying made it clear he hadn't a clue what to do with a daughter in tears.

"Um, a little. I'm really looking forward to moving to Wyneheart and spending time with you, but I'm also going to miss Honey."

"I see. Do you always cry when you move?"

"No." She never cried. Ever. Well, hardly ever. The only other time she could remember crying was when her mother passed away. But moving never made her cry. It mostly filled her with anticipation, not with sorrow.

"So this Honey is a special town?"

She thought about that. Yes, Honey was special, at

least it was to her. She'd met a lot of terrific people here, many of whom she considered friends.

And she was definitely going to miss Rufus. Saying hi to him on the way by each morning while she was jogging was one of the bright spots of her day. In fact, she was almost convinced that sooner or later, Rufus would actually wag his tail for her. It could be wishful thinking, of course, but she couldn't shake the feeling that it was a possibility.

"Emma, are you still there?" her father asked.

"Yes. And yes, Honey is special."

"I see. Well, Wyneheart is a special town as well. Filled with very charming people."

Emma sighed. Charming. Yes, she was sure Wyneheart had charming residents. But they weren't charming in the way that Nathan was. The man could charm the snow out of the sky on an August afternoon.

"I sense there's more to your sadness than missing Honey. Want to tell me what's really wrong?"

Despite Leigh's suggestion, Emma hadn't intended on pouring her heart out to her father, but the next thing she knew, she blurted, "I'm in love with Nathan Barrett."

"I see."

"And his company is the only reason the town of Honey is still thriving. If he were to move his business, the town would be reduced to tumbleweeds."

"I see."

"So he can't possibly follow me."

"I see."

"And if I stay here, then I don't get to teach at Wyneheart or spend time with you."

"I see."

Emma sighed. "But even though I know leaving here is the right decision, I can't seem to stop crying."

"I see."

Despite how upset she was, Emma sighed. Her father was trying, but she had to admit, he was really bad at this comforting thing.

"Anyway, Dad, that's why I'm crying. But I guess in time I'll feel better," she admitted. "I'm just down right now."

"Nonsense."

Okay, she'd accepted that he wasn't good at comforting, but calling her emotions nonsense seemed a trifle harsh.

"I'm not usually so weepy about things," she said in her own defense.

"No, I didn't mean how you felt was nonsense; I meant your plan."

Emma frowned. "Dad, I think maybe I should just call back later."

"No. I need to tell you something that will make you feel much better. I love you, Emma."

Well, that did make her feel somewhat better. She liked knowing she had her father's love. "I love you, too, Dad."

"Good. Then there's something you can do for me."

"What?"

"Stay in Honey with Nathan."

She blinked. "But, Dad, what about you and the job and my future?"

"I never got the chance to be much of a father to you when you were growing up, Emma. I've always regretted that. But today, I'm getting my chance. The most important thing in the world to me is that you're happy. And dear, love is too precious to walk away from. If you really love Nathan, you should be with him. Now I'll finally have a reason to use those frequent flyer miles I've been accruing. I'll come visit, quite often as a matter of fact. And you have to promise to come visit me as well."

"But what about the job you had lined up for me?"

"You're very smart. You can find another one at the University of Texas or any of the other colleges around. I'll help you in any way I can."

Emma felt more tears trickle down her cheeks. She couldn't believe how sweet her father was. How had she been so blessed to have two great men in her life?

"Emma, dear, are you crying again?"

"I love you, Dad."

"I love you, too. Now go find Nathan, ask him to marry you, then get on a flight to Massachusetts and introduce me to him. I never got to play the part of a stern father interrogating his daughter's beau. I don't want to miss my chance."

Emma laughed, knowing her father was going to love Nathan as much as she did.

"Thank you," she said softly.

"Just don't be surprised if I also find myself a teaching position in Texas. I want to be around when the grandchildren arrive."

Emma felt more tears come, and this time she didn't even try to stop them. Her life had suddenly become too wonderful for words.

"You're an idiot," Leigh said the second she walked into Nathan's office.

"If I agree, will you go home?"

She rolled her eyes. "As if. Now what are you going to do about this?"

Nathan held on to the slim hope that his sister wasn't talking about his relationship with Emma. "What am I going to do about what?"

"You know good and well about what. Emma. You. The fact that even Rufus is smart enough to know the two of you belong together. So why are you letting her leave?"

Nathan had asked himself the same question a million times even though he knew the answer.

"Not that it's any of your business, but I can't ask Emma to give up her future and stay here. And I can't very well go with her since that would mean the end of Barrett Software."

Leigh sighed. "Jeez, Nathan, you have the most complicated problems. Okay, I'll admit you'd be a real jerk if you asked her to stay. But would the company really fold if you lived someplace else?"

Unfortunately, the past few weeks had shown him what a vital part he was to the company. When Simplify had run into problems, he'd done everything from some coding to helping with design problems and finally pitching in on the testing.

"Yes. Barrett Software needs me."

"Can't the company come with you? Can't you relocate?"

Nathan gave his sister a pointed look. "And what would this town do for revenue? A large portion of the town works for me."

"Okay. Okay. But what if you sell the company to someone else?"

"What if that someone else moves the company?"

Leigh groaned and slapped his desk. "Stop finding negatives. Look for positives."

He felt compelled to point out, "There aren't a lot of positives, Leigh."

"There's the most important positive—you and Emma love each other."

"You seem awfully certain of that."

Leigh nodded. "I am."

Nathan smiled at his sister's confidence. "You sure you're not just trying to get me so distracted that I'll leave you alone?"

She grinned. "I'll admit, it's a definite upside. But seriously, I'm glad you found someone perfect for you. Now stop being such an idiot and work this out. You're a smart guy. You solve big problems every day. You need to solve this one, too. Don't let her get away, Nathan. You know you'll never find someone like her again." Finally, she added softly, "She's really leaving, Nathan. You can't let that happen."

Nathan knew his sister was right. He couldn't let Emma leave, at least not alone. He needed her in his life. As much as it seemed selfish to sell the company just so he could be with the woman he loved, he also knew he'd regret it forever if he didn't do everything in his power to make things work with Emma.

He'd just have to make absolutely certain that whatever company he sold Barrett Software to would treat the employees right and leave the headquarters here in Honey. If he handled this correctly, he could have Emma in his life without destroying the town or the lives of the people who worked for him. Sure, he'd miss Barrett Software. He'd miss it a lot.

But not as much as he'd miss Emma if he let her leave.

"I'll find a buyer for the company," he announced to his sister. "Of course, they'll have to promise to keep it based here in Honey, so it may take me a little while. But you're right. I can't let Emma out of my life."

"Now you're talking," Leigh said with a grin. "So go tell Emma before she heads back to Austin."

By the time Leigh finished speaking, Nathan was already halfway to the door.

੪

EMMA WAS ALL SET TO GO FIND NATHAN WHEN THERE was a knock at her door. A thrill of excitement danced through her, and she knew before she even opened the door that this time, it was Nathan.

"Hi," she said after opening the door.

He grinned and leaned against the doorjamb.

"Hi, yourself. Guess what?"

"Wait. I have something to tell you," she said, anticipation bubbling inside of her.

"Nope, sorry, but this time I'm not doing ladies first. I need to tell you my news before you can tell me your news."

She couldn't keep herself from smiling. "I thought you were raised better than that."

"No. That's just a rumor." He glanced beyond her. "May I come inside?"

"You own the place." She pushed the door open wider. "Make yourself at home."

He walked past her and sat on the couch. Emma barely kept from hugging him on the way by. But she'd let him tell her his news first. It wouldn't be easy to wait, but she'd do it. She settled next to him and smiled.

"So, what do you want to tell me?"

"I've decided to sell Barrett Software."

Emma couldn't believe what she was hearing. "But what about the employees? What about Honey?"

"I'll find a company to buy me out that will promise not to move the headquarters."

"You can make such stipulations?"

He nodded. "Pretty much."

"You don't sound very positive."

"Emma, don't you see? This way we can be together."

She couldn't believe how much he loved her. He was willing to sell Barrett Software and move away from Honey just to be with her. "You'd really do all that? For me?"

He leaned over and kissed her deeply. "You mean everything to me. I'll do whatever is necessary to keep you in my life."

Emma blinked back tears of joy. "Really? Because I feel the same way. And as much as I appreciate your willingness to sell your company, it won't be necessary.

One of the things I love about you is how loyal you are to your family and to Honey."

"I'll make certain they're both fine before I leave for Massachusetts," he assured her. "I want to be with you."

"Nathan, you can't take the risk that your employees would have to move. Even if you got promises in writing from the buyer, something could go wrong."

He took one of her hands in his own. "I'll make certain nothing goes wrong. I promise."

She shook her head. "That's not good enough. If the new owners decided to move, you couldn't stop them. Then what would happen to Honey? To the employees? To Rufus? Let's face it, we know it's almost impossible to move him."

"That won't happen," he assured her again. "And not just because it would be impossible to move Rufus. Because I'd never let anything bad happen to this town."

She placed one hand on the side of his face, loving him, loving being able to touch him like this. "That's exactly why we're not going to Massachusetts. I spoke to my father, and he agrees with me. I can find another job at a university close to Honey. And we can visit Dad often, and he'll visit us. But..."

He raised one eyebrow. "But?"

"I can never find another man as wonderful as you."

Again, he leaned over and kissed her. This time, the kiss caught fire, and Emma suggested, "Want to move to the bed and continue this discussion?"

Nathan pretended to be shocked. "Ms. Montgomery, what sort of man do you think I am?"

"A wonderful, terrific, magnificent, fantastic man who I hope to spend the rest of my life with."

He brushed her lips with his. "And you're the most amazing, fascinating, exciting woman I've ever met. Will you marry me?"

"Yes," she said on a sigh.

He kissed her hand. "I promise you, Emma, that I'll do whatever it takes to make all of your dreams come true. I won't let you down."

"Same back at you, hotshot," she said, knowing their life together was going to be filled with love and hope and promise. They would work together to make certain they both got what they wanted and needed from life.

This time when he kissed her, she wrapped her arms around him and held him tight, unable to believe how lucky she was.

"Wow," Nathan said when they finally ended the kiss. "That was something else."

"Honey, you ain't seen nothing yet," she teased.

Nathan had a definite twinkle in his eyes. "Hey, is that any way for an English major to talk?"

"It's perfectly acceptable if she's an English major in love," Emma said. "And I am most definitely an English major in love."

DEAR READER,

Readers are an author's life blood and the stories couldn't happen without *you*. Thank you so much for reading! If you enjoyed *Handsome Boss,* we would so appreciate a review. You have no idea how much it means to us.

If you'd like to keep up with our latest releases, you can sign up for our newsletter @ https://loriwilde.com/sign-up/.

Please turn the page for an excerpt of the next book in the The Handsome Devil series, *Handsome Lawman*.

To check out our other books, you can visit us on the web @ www.loriwilde.com.

EXCERPT: HANDSOME LAWMAN

"Trent Barrett, I insist you arrest Erin Weber immediately. The woman is a thief and belongs in jail," Delia Haverhill hollered, her arms crossed under her ample chest. "Arrest her right now."

Trent scratched his jaw and considered the middle-aged woman in front of him. Delia wasn't what you would call the sweetest person in Honey, Texas. Truth be told, she put the cur in curmudgeon.

But still, as chief of police of Honey, he couldn't simply ignore Delia's complaint. And the woman hadn't, to his knowledge, ever had anyone arrested before. There very well could be some truth in what she was saying. A least a little.

"Why don't you tell me what the problem is and who Erin Weber might be," he said in a calm, soft voice, hoping Delia might follow suit and stop hollering at the top of her lungs. "Then we can figure out what's the best course of action to take."

Unfortunately, Delia didn't lower her volume one

bit. She leaned halfway across his desk and said, "I've already told you what action needs to be taken. Erin Weber needs to be arrested. Now get up from behind that desk and come with me. I'll show you who this woman is and what she did. You won't believe her nerve. I was nice enough to visit her store last Saturday with my grandson, and she rewards me by stealing my Pookie. And to make it worse, she's displaying Pookie right outside her store. The woman belongs in jail, I tell you." Trent thought he was up to date on all the street names for drugs, but he'd never heard of pookie. "What in the world is pookie?"

Delia wagged a finger at him. "Get out of your chair, and I'll show you."

Reluctantly, Trent stood. "I'll be happy to get one of my officers to help you, Delia. But I have a meeting with the mayor in about an hour."

Delia frowned. "Did I or did I not change your diapers when you were too young to know your feet from your hands?"

His secretary, Ann Seaver, had walked in midway through Delia's comment. She raised one eyebrow and looked precariously close to giggling.

Trent shook his head and sighed. "Delia, I sure do hope you're talking about when you used to babysit me decades ago. If you mean something else, then one of us is seriously warped."

Delia was obviously not amused. She looked at Trent like he was something stuck on the bottom of her shoes. "Of course I'm talking about when I babysat you. And I would think that means you'll be happy to help me now."

She gave him a squinty-eyed look. "After all, I never let you cry yourself to sleep like some babysitters do. I rocked you to sleep and sang you pretty songs."

Ann made a spurting sound behind the hand she had across her mouth. Trent was certain she wasn't the only one who would be laughing today about what Delia had said. No doubt Ann would tell most of the officers, and by the end of the day, everyone would be quoting Delia Haverhill.

Dang it all.

"Come on, Delia. Show me what this pookie is." He circled his desk and stood next to the older woman. "I think you've already shared enough babysitting stories for one day."

Delia didn't even crack a smile. She simply nodded and headed toward the door. When they drew even with Ann, his secretary was still laughing.

"What in the world are you laughing about, young lady?" Delia asked her. "Seems to me I changed more than a few of your diapers, too."

Ann turned bright red, and Trent chuckled as he trailed after Delia. That was one major advantage of growing up in a small town. Sure, everyone knew embarrassing things about you. But hey, you knew embarrassing things about them as well.

"So, Delia, how long do you expect this to take?" he had to ask as they headed for the front door.

"It will take however long you need to read Erin Weber her Melissa rights."

The bright sunshine hit him once they were outside, so Trent pulled his sunglasses out of his pocket and slipped them on. "Miranda."

"What?"

"Not Melissa. Miranda."

Delia waved one hand and started down the street. "Melissa. Miranda. What difference does it make? Just read her the rights and toss her in jail. Now come on."

Reluctantly, Trent followed. He sure didn't like being ordered around, but as the chief of police, he had to keep the people of Honey happy.

"Tell me, what is this pookie stuff you think some woman stole from you?" he asked once they were headed down Main Street.

"First off, it isn't pookie stuff. His name is Pookie. Pay attention, Trent."

He thought he had been, but reading smoke signals would be easier than understanding Delia Haverhill. "Sorry if I misunderstood."

"Second off, it isn't just some woman who stole my Pookie. It's Erin Weber, the woman who opened the pet shop over on Collier Street. Naturally, I suspected her as soon as Pookie disappeared."

By now, he and Delia had turned off Main Street and were halfway down Collier. Delia pointed to the front door of a store.

"There's Pookie. Big as life. On display for the whole town to see. Erin certainly has some nerve."

Trent looked where she was pointing and bit back a grin. Pookie was a plastic statue of a rabbit, the kind you might put in your garden or flowerbed. The statue was old and well-worn and couldn't be worth more than a couple of bucks.

But Delia was cooing and fussing over the blasted thing like it was real.

"Now go on inside and arrest her," Delia said.

Trent slipped off his sunglasses and glanced around. As he could have predicted, he and Delia were starting to draw a crowd. Honey didn't offer a lot of diversions, so anytime anything even moderately interesting happened, everyone rushed out to see what was going on. He better head on in and talk to this Erin Weber before he found himself knee-deep in nosy citizens.

"Arrest her, arrest her, arrest her," Delia said loudly. Then she folded her arms under her ample chest once more and took on the expression of one who believes herself incapable of error.

Damn, what a way to start the day.

With about as much enthusiasm as a ten-year-old boy stuck at a Girl Scout meeting, Trent shoved open the door of Precious Pets and walked inside.

He'd only made it a few steps when a woman yelled, "Freeze!"

Trent froze as instructed and started to go for his gun when a petite, brown-haired dynamo rushed at him from the back of the store.

"Don't move or you'll frighten Brutus," the woman said. "You almost stepped on him. He's right by your left foot." She tipped her head, her expression more than a little accusatory. "He just escaped from the bath. Didn't you see Brutus when you came in?"

Obviously not or he wouldn't have almost stepped on him. Trent glanced around and didn't immediately see anything. But after learning what a Pookie was, Trent wasn't certain he wanted to know what a Brutus might be. Probably a big ol' ugly snake. Or maybe a tarantula.

But curiosity got to him, so he looked down anyway, then breathed a sigh of relief.

Brutus was a little bitty fluffball.

"What kind of animal is that?" he had to ask.

The woman frowned. "A puppy, of course. What in the world did you think he was?"

Trent studied the round, white ball of fur with two black specks for eyes. "He kinda looks like a dust bunny."

The woman moved forward and picked up the puppy off the floor. "A dust bunny. Sheesh. He's a sweet-heart, aren't you, baby?"

Obviously knowing he was being praised, Brutus let out a series of yips and yaps. Trent would give the puppy credit—he had an impressive bark for something that looked like a ball of lint. No wonder the dog had a tough name like Brutus. He needed every advantage he could get.

"Is there something I can help you with?" the woman asked, still cradling the dog.

"I'm Trent Barrett, chief of police here in Honey." He extended his hand, which the woman shook in a firm, no-nonsense handshake. Just like the pup, the woman might look small and fragile, but she was stronger than she appeared. Her grip would do a lumberjack proud.

"I'm Erin Weber. I own Precious Pets." Brutus started squirming, so Erin put the puppy down. The furball immediately trotted over and tugged on Trent's shoelaces.

"Hey, mutt, cut it out," he said.

"Brutus might not be a pedigree, but he's hardly a mutt," Erin defended. "He's a rescue."

"I didn't mean mutt in a negative way."

"Mutt is a word that has no positive connotations," she countered. "Even though he's from the animal shelter, Brutus has a great deal of dignity." Trent grinned as he watched the pup chew on the shoelaces of his best boots. "Is that a fact? He has dignity?"

Erin frowned. "Of course."

Trent tried to wipe the grin off his face, but the dang thing refused to budge. "I'll keep that in mind."

There was a loud rapping on the front door, then Delia hollered, "Have you arrested her yet?"

Erin frowned. "Who's that?"

"Delia Haverhill. Do you know her?"

"Yes. I met her last weekend. Who does she want you to arrest?"

Brutus had settled down on one of Trent's shoes, apparently to take a nap, so Trent bent down and scooped him up. The dog panted and yipped at him and looked like he might leak from either end, so Trent handed Brutus back to Erin.

"Arrest her, Trent. Do it right now," Delia continued hollering through the door. "How dare she take Pookie!"

Erin was staring at the door to her shop, obviously befuddled. "Um, what does she—"

Trent blew out a sigh. "I'm afraid Delia wants me to arrest you for stealing her Pookie."

**

Erin couldn't have heard this man correctly. There

was absolutely no way she could have heard him correctly. No one had a reason to want her arrested.

Pushing away her initial panic, she politely asked, "Excuse me? Did you say you're arresting me?"

Trent Barrett smiled, a slow, sexy, lady-killer smile. Erin absolutely refused to react to his smile. Her days of falling for handsome but unreliable men were over. So what if he was tall, with deep-black hair and the most amazing blue eyes? He wasn't her type. Nope. Not at all.

And even if he was her type—which he wasn't—she could hardly be attracted to a man who might arrest her.

"I said Delia wants me to arrest you, but I'm only here to ask a couple of questions," he explained.

The woman outside the front door banged on the glass again. "I'm serious, Trent; I expect results."

Confrontation in any form always made Erin uncomfortable—at least it used to. But since her wedding day fiasco, she'd worked hard at becoming more assertive. These days, she really tried to stand up for herself. She couldn't imagine what she had done to Delia Haverhill that had made her so angry, but Erin wasn't about to be intimidated either by the handsome chief of police or the irate woman outside.

"Look, Chief Barrett—"

"Trent," he said.

Erin shook her head. "No, I'll call you Chief Barrett, if you don't mind."

Once again, he flashed a flirty grin that Erin suspected usually reduced any female within a two-mile radius into a fluttery mass of jelly. Too bad for the chief that she was now flutter-proof. Okay, not one hundred percent flutter-proof but close to it.

"So, Chief Barrett, whatever Delia thinks I've done, I haven't. I have never broken the law."

"I appreciate that, Ms. Weber. Delia is upset about Pookie."

Erin took a deep, calming breath and tried again. "You said that pookie thing before. What in the world is a pookie?"

He chuckled, the sound deep and inviting, but Erin ignored it. Well, tried to, and came pretty darn close.

"Pookie is the name of Delia's plastic rabbit which used to reside in her garden and is now sitting in front of your store. Delia seems to think you had something to do with Pookie's relocation."

"That's the silliest thing I've ever heard. I have no idea what you're talking about. Let me put Brutus in his carrier, then I want to see this Pookie."

Trent nodded. "Seems like the best approach, but I'll warn you, Delia's a trifle hot under the collar. I'm going to head on outside and give her a couple of pointers on police protocol."

Erin had to ask, "Such as?"

"Mostly that she's not allowed to scream and yell while you and I are chatting."

"I don't think you should call interrogating me about a plastic rabbit chatting, Chief."

"I don't think you should call what I'm going to be doing interrogating, Ms. Weber."

Erin didn't want to soften toward Trent Barrett, for a lot of reasons, but she had to admit, he hadn't done anything too terrible. At least not so far.

"I'll put Brutus in his carrier and be outside in a sec," she repeated, not as nervous as she'd been before.

"I'll go talk to Delia."

Although Brutus didn't appreciate being put into his dog carrier, he accepted his fate with as much good grace as a feisty puppy could manage. Then Erin smoothed her green T-shirt that read Precious Pets and her beige slacks.

She took a series of calming breaths following the techniques she'd read about to reduce tension and said the affirmations the book had advised: "You're powerful. You're strong. You're filled with energy."

Then she headed to the front door, her steps decisive, her head held high. She'd just moved to this town and opened her business. Sure, the people of Honey didn't know her. But she wasn't a thief, and Delia Haverhill was about to learn that fact.

Feeling ready, Erin stepped outside and noticed two things—first, that Trent must have had a really intense talking to with Delia, because the older woman had her mouth clamped shut and looked about to explode.

And second, she noticed that Pookie was one sad and sorry-looking plastic bunny rabbit.

Going on the offensive, Erin said to Delia, "I'm so sorry about what happened to you, but I didn't take your rabbit. I have no idea how it came to be in front of my store. But I'm glad you found it and can put it back in your garden."

Delia continued to glare. "If you didn't put it there, who did?"

"Ah, but if I'd stolen it, why would I display it in

front of my store where you'd readily see it? Wouldn't I hide Pookie so I could keep him?"

A tiny fragment of doubt crossed the older woman's face. Erin knew Delia was now a little less sure.

"Delia," Trent said softly. "Remember what we talked about before you say anything."

Delia eventually made a noise that sounded like "hmmrrphfft" but didn't say anything else. Erin frankly couldn't tell if that was a good hmmrrphfft or a bad hmmrrphfft, but at least Delia had stopped demanding that Erin be arrested.

Now Erin turned her attention to Trent, needing his help to solve this mystery. "Honestly, I have no idea how that statue—"

"Pookie," Delia said. "His name is Pookie."

Erin nodded. "Right. Pookie. Well, anyway, I have no idea how Pookie came to be in front of my store."

"You have to know something," Delia said. "Did you see anyone lurking around?"

"Delia," Trent said again, raising one eyebrow and giving the woman a look that Erin could only call marginally polite. "I'm sure if Ms. Weber had seen anyone lurking, she would have called the police whether or not they'd been carrying a pookie."

"Hmmrrphfft," Delia said again.

"You didn't notice Pookie outside when you came to work this morning?" Trent asked.

Erin only wished she had. Although, truthfully, even if she had seen Pookie, she probably wouldn't have called the police to report a plastic bunny. "I didn't see it because I live in the apartment above my shop. I don't come in through the front door. I come down the back stairs."

While Trent wrote a few things in a small notebook, Erin looked at Delia. She felt sorry for the older woman. Delia was obviously very upset. "Delia, I want you to know I would never steal Pookie. I know what it's like to have people take things that belong to you. I can imagine how upset you were when you discovered Pookie missing. He's such an...er...um, attractive rabbit. He must bring you a great deal of joy."

Delia's expression softened, but just a minuscule amount. She still pretty much looked like she wanted Erin beheaded.

"Yes, Pookie is dear to me," Delia said.

Erin reached out and patted the battered plastic animal. "He's sweet. You must have missed him."

Delia held the statue close. "He is sweet, which is why someone stole him."

Erin deliberately ignored the baiting tone in the woman's voice. Instead, she said, "I'm so glad you got him back. When I was in first grade, one of the boys stole my lunch box, which I loved. I was devastated. I ran home and cried and cried."

Delia's expression softened a little more around the edges. "What kind of lunch box was it?"

"Scooby-Doo. And I loved that lunch box. I was so proud of it. I couldn't believe it was gone."

Delia nodded. "Scooby-Doo is a good choice. So, did you get the lunch box back?"

"No. Although I knew who took it, no one would believe me. My parents said I'd probably lost it on the bus and wouldn't buy me another because they felt I'd been careless. My teacher said I'd probably lost it at home somewhere and didn't believe me when I said Billy Porter had stolen it."

"You poor thing," Delia said, patting her on the arm.

"The worst part was that a couple of months later, Billy started coming to school carrying the Scooby-Doo lunch box. I could even see where he'd marked out my name and written his own. I was so upset, but no one would do anything, so I had to ignore it. But it was hard to ignore since Billy liked to tease me by saying 'Don't you wish you had a lunch box as nice as mine?'"

"That rat," Delia huffed. "Someone should have taught that boy a lesson."

Erin looked Delia directly in the eye. "I agree. What Billy did was horrible. That's why I would never, ever take something that didn't belong to me. As you can tell, I still to this day remember the Scooby-Doo lunch box incident."

Delia patted her arm again. "You poor thing."

Trent cleared his throat. "Excuse me, but, Ms. Weber, do you have any idea who might have left Pookie outside your store?"

Delia spun around and glared at him, her hands on her wide hips. "Trent Barrett, have you no manners?"

Both Trent and Erin looked at each other. He seemed as baffled by Delia's comment as she was.

Trent explained. "Delia, I'm trying to find out about Pookie. I thought that was what you wanted me to do."

Delia pointed one finger at him. "You should have sympathized about the lunch box first. Then you can ask about Pookie."

Trent turned to Erin, his deep-blue eyes sparkling

with humor. She could tell he was trying hard not to smile. To his credit, he managed to look sincere when he said, "My deepest apologies," he said. "I'm so sorry to hear about your loss."

"Thank you." Now Erin had to keep from smiling at the mischievous look in Trent's eyes. The man was a flirt, plain and simple. She could tell from the way he was looking at her that he found her attractive.

"Now that I've paid my respects to your lost Scooby-Doo lunch box, do you have any idea how Pookie came to be outside your store?" he asked.

"None at all," she admitted and glanced at Delia. "I really am sorry this happened to you."

Delia patted her arm yet again. "I appreciate your concern. And I realize now that you couldn't possibly have had anything to do with Pookie's disappearance. Not when you've suffered yourself. Trent will have to figure out who really did it."

Erin was relieved the other woman believed her. Not only would she hate to think someone blamed her for a theft, but it wouldn't do Precious Pets any good if everyone started thinking badly of her.

"I'm not done asking questions," Trent said to Delia.

Delia shook her head. "No more questions. She didn't do it. Enough said. Go on back to your office and arrest someone else. I'm going to visit with Erin for a bit." She glanced at the store. "Do you let the local shelters list dogs and cats so they can find forever homes? I didn't pay that much attention when I was here with my grandson last Saturday. You remember Zach, don't you?"

Erin smiled. It would be difficult to forget the eight-year-old. He'd asked a million questions while Delia had visited with the mayor and his wife.

"Yes, I remember Zach. Yes, I help the local animal shelter find homes for the strays. A couple times a month, they bring a few of their pets here to see if my customers are interested in adopting. And then sometimes, I act as a foster home to a kitten or a puppy. Right now, I'm taking care of a puppy named Brutus. He's a sweetie and needs a good home."

"Let me take a look at him. Also, do you sell birdseed? I have a new bird feeder that looks like the Tower of Pisa. I need to stock it."

Erin smiled, relaxing for the first time since this whole mess had started. Even though she knew all along that she hadn't done a thing wrong, just the threat of being arrested made her jittery and jumpy. She was used to always being the good girl. The good daughter. The good student. The good fiancée.

She wouldn't know how to be bad if someone gave her lessons.

"I have several types of birdseed," Erin told Delia, thrilled the woman was now being friendly. "I'm certain I have something that will work for you."

She turned to look at the handsome chief of police. Her pulse rate picked up, but she ignored it. Even Pookie, the plastic bunny rabbit statue, was smart enough to know a man like Trent Barrett was trouble.

"Are we done?" she asked him.

He grinned, his look downright flirtatious. His blue eyes sparkled once again with mischief, and Erin's first instinct was to smile back at him. Thankfully, her common sense kicked in, and she stopped herself.

Smiling at Trent struck her as an activity only a tiny bit less dangerous than carrying around a lit stick of dynamite. The man was a handsome devil all right.

When she didn't return his smile, he only grinned bigger. She could tell he found her amusing, but she didn't care. She wasn't going to flirt with this man no matter how tempting it might be.

"You're no longer a suspect in Pookie's kidnapping," Trent finally said. "But I'd say we're far from done."

With that and a goodbye to Delia, he walked away. Erin frowned. What did he mean by that crack that they were far from done?

"Woo-wee, that boy is a charmer. All of those Barrett boys are," Delia said as they watched Trent Barrett leave. "But that one, he's a flirt through and through. A mighty fine-looking man, but a flirt, that's for sure."

"Mmm." Erin didn't want to discuss Trent Barrett. The man made her...pensive. And pensive could be bad for her emotional health.

Delia yanked open the door to the shop and headed straight for the birdseed. "You have a wonderful selection."

"Thanks." Erin helped her pick just the right type for the birds she wanted to attract. Then after introducing Delia to Brutus, she rang up the older woman's order.

"Sure you don't want to adopt this puppy? He's a great little fellow," Erin tried, even though Delia had already made it clear she thought Brutus was way too active.

"Brutus isn't right for me. Does he have any sisters?"

Erin hid her disappointment. Delia wasn't the first person to ask that. So far, Erin had sent three people to the county animal shelter to see Brutus' sisters.

Well, an adopted animal was one more with a home, so Erin told Delia, "Yes. The shelter has several females left from the litter."

Delia eyed Brutus, who was now gnawing on Erin's sneaker. "Yes, I think one of the girls might suit me better. I'll go over there this afternoon."

Erin reached down and detached Brutus from her shoe, telling him firmly, "No, Brutus." Then she said to Delia, "I'm sure you'll find a wonderful dog to love."

"I'm sure I will, too." Just as the older woman was about to leave, she said, "Hon, before I go, I wanted to say I'm so sorry about the mix-up this morning. I only hope Trent finds the people who stole Pookie. They deserve to be in jail."

"I'm sure the chief will do a thorough investigation," Erin assured her.

"You're probably right. Even though he's something of a rogue, Trent's good at his job. He keeps this town running smoothly." She leaned forward a little and added, "But just so you know, be very careful if you decide to go out with him. That man breaks hearts as easily as I crack eggs."

Erin handed Delia the bag with the birdseed and said as much to herself as to the other woman, "I'm not worried. My heart is unbreakable."

EXCERPT: HANDSOME RANCHER

Don't miss the first book in the Handsome Devil series. Order now.

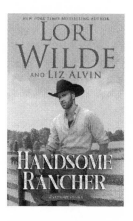

As she studied him, standing near the entrance to the city council room, Megan Kendall couldn't help thinking what a handsome devil Chase Barrett was.

Everyone in the small town of Honey, Texas, thought so as well. With his drop-dead gorgeous looks and his handsome-devil smile, women fell for him like pine trees knocked down by a powerful tornado.

Even Megan couldn't claim to be immune. She and Chase had been good friends for over twenty years, and he still didn't know she was madly in love with him.

Yep, he was a handsome devil all right.

"Picture him naked," Leigh Barrett whispered to Megan.

Stunned, Megan turned to stare at Chase's younger sister. "Excuse me?"

Thankfully, Leigh nodded toward the front of the room instead of in her brother's direction. "The mayor. When you're giving your presentation, if you get nervous, picture him naked."

Megan slipped her glasses down her nose and studied Earl Guthrie, the seventy-three-year-old mayor of Honey. When Earl caught her gaze, he gave Megan a benign, vague smile.

"I don't think so," Megan said to Leigh. "I prefer to think of Earl as fully clothed."

Leigh giggled. "Okay, maybe that wasn't such a hot idea after all. Let me see if I can find someone else for you to think of naked."

"That's not necessary. I'm not nervous." Megan flipped through her index cards.

Her argument was flawless, her plan foolproof. She had nothing to be nervous about. Besides, as the head librarian of the Honey Library, she knew every person in the room. This presentation would be a snap.

But with puppy-like enthusiasm, Leigh had already stood and was looking around. She hadn't spotted her oldest brother yet, but Megan knew it was only a matter of time before she did.

"Leigh, I'm fine," Megan tried, but Leigh finally saw Chase and yelled at him to come over and join them.

Chase made his way through the crowded room. The city council meetings usually drew a big audience, but Megan was happy to see even more people than usual had turned out to listen to her presentation of fundraiser ideas for new playground equipment.

When Chase got even with Megan and Leigh, he leaned across Megan to ruffle his sister's dark hair. Then he dropped into the folding chair next to Megan and winked at her. "Ladies, how are you tonight?"

Megan tried to keep her expression pleasant, but it wasn't easy. Ever since she'd moved back to Honey last year, pretending her feelings for Chase were platonic was proving harder and harder. At six-two, with deep black hair and even deeper blue eyes, he made her heart race and her palms sweat.

"Don't ruffle my hair, bozo." Leigh huffed at Megan's right, smoothing her hair. "I'm in college. I'm too old to have my hair ruffled."

To Megan's left, Chase chuckled. "Squirt, you're never going to be too old for me to ruffle your hair. When you're eighty, I'm going to totter up to you and do it."

"You and what orderly?" Leigh teased. "And just for the record, I like Nathan and Trent much better than I like you."

"Oh, please." Megan rolled her eyes at that one. Leigh loved all of her brothers, but everyone knew

Chase was her favorite. When she was home from college, she always stayed with Chase.

"I love you, too, squirt," Chase said, not rising to his sister's taunt. Instead, he nudged Megan. "You okay?"

"I told her to imagine the mayor naked if she got nervous, but she doesn't want to do that," Leigh supplied.

"I can see why not," Chase said. "Earl's not exactly stud-muffin material."

"Oooh, I know what she should do." Leigh practically bounced in her chair. "Megan, if you get nervous, picture Chase naked."

Megan froze and willed herself to stay calm. The absolute last thing she wanted to think about was Chase naked. Okay, maybe she did want to think of him naked, but not right now. Not right before she had to speak in front of a large portion of the entire town.

"I don't think so," Megan muttered, shooting a glare at Leigh.

The younger woman knew how Megan felt about her brother, and this was simply one more not-so-subtle attempt to get the two of them together. In the past few months, Leigh's matchmaking maneuvers had grown more extreme.

"I don't think I'll need to picture anyone naked," Megan stated.

On her other side, Chase offered, "Well, if you get flustered and it will make things easier for you, you go ahead and think of me naked, Megan. Whatever I can do to help."

Megan knew Chase was teasing her, but suddenly

she realized how many years she'd wasted waiting for him to take her seriously.

She'd fallen for him when she'd moved to town at eight. Dreamed about him since she'd turned sixteen. And tried like the dickens to forget him when she'd been away at college and then later working at a library in Dallas for five years.

But nothing had helped. Not even seriously dating a man in Dallas had helped. In her soul, Megan believed she and Chase were meant to be together.

If only she could get him to notice her.

"Hey there, Chase," a smooth, feline voice fairly purred over their shoulders. "You're looking yummy. Like an especially luscious dessert, and I positively love dessert."

Oh, great. Megan glanced behind her. Janet Defries. Just what she needed tonight.

Chase smiled at the woman half leaning on his chair. "Hey, Janet. Do you plan on helping Megan with her committee?"

From the look on Janet's face, the only thing she planned on helping herself to was Chase, served on a platter.

She leaned toward Chase, the position no doubt deliberate since a generous amount of cleavage was exposed. "Are you going to help with this committee, Chase? Because if you are, I might be able to pry free a few hours."

Yeah, right. Megan shared a glance with Leigh. They both knew Janet would no more help with the committee than dogs would sing.

"I'd like to help, but it's a busy time on the ranch," Chase said.

"Shame." Janet slipped into the chair directly behind him. "I think you and I should figure out a way to spend some quality time together."

Her message couldn't have been clearer if she'd plastered it on a billboard. Megan hated herself for wanting to know, but she couldn't not look. She turned to see what Chase's reaction was to the woman's blatant come-on.

Mild interest. Megan repressed a sigh. Of course. Janet was exactly the type of woman Chase favored. One with a high-octane body and zero interest in a lasting relationship.

"Maybe we'll figure it out one of these days," Chase said, and Megan felt her temperature climb.

Okay, so she didn't have a drawer at home full of D-cups, but Megan knew she could make Chase happy. She could make him believe in love again.

If the dimwit would give her the chance.

Janet placed one hand on Chase's arm and licked her lips. "Well, you hurry up, else I might decide to go after Nathan or Trent instead. You're not the only handsome fella in your family."

Chase chuckled as he faced forward in his chair once again. "I sure am being threatened with my brothers tonight. But I'd like to point out that neither of them stopped by to lend their support, and I'm sitting here like an angel."

Leigh snorted. "Angel? You? Give me a break. You could make the devil himself blush, Chase Barrett."

Chase's grin was pure male satisfaction. "I do my best."

As Megan knew only too well. She'd watched him beguile a large percentage of the females in this part of Texas. Why couldn't he throw a little of that wickedness her way? Just once, she'd like to show him how combustible they could be together.

But even though she'd been back in Honey for almost a year, the man still treated her like a teenager. She'd just celebrated her twenty-ninth birthday. She wasn't a sheltered virgin with fairy-tale dreams of romance. She was a flesh and blood woman who knew what she wanted out of life.

She wanted Chase.

After a great deal of commotion getting the microphone to the right level, the mayor finally started the meeting. Within a few minutes, it was time for her presentation. Megan stood, adjusting her glasses.

"Remember, picture Chase naked if you get nervous," Leigh whispered but not very softly.

Megan was in the process of scooting past Chase, who had stood to let her by. She froze, standing directly in front of the man who consumed her dreams and starred in her fantasies.

He grinned.

"You know, I think I just may do that," Megan said. "And if he gets nervous, he can picture me naked, too."

❧

Had to be the heat, Chase decided as he settled back in the wobbly folding chair. Or maybe the water. Either way, something was weird because Megan Kendall had just flirted with him.

Leigh moved over to sit in the chair next to Chase. "You talk to Nathan or Trent today?"

Chase glanced at Megan, who was straightening her notes, so he had a couple of seconds to answer his sister. "Nathan and all of his employees are working overtime trying to get that computer program done. Trent has a new officer who joined the force today, so he's busy, too. You're stuck with me."

Rather than looking upset, Leigh's expression was downright blissful. "Megan and I are thrilled you're here."

Through narrowed eyes, Chase studied his sister. She was up to something as sure as the sun rose in the east, and he'd bet his prize bull it had something to do with him breaking up her necking session with Billy Joe Tate last night.

"Whatever you're doing, stop it," Chase told her. "It won't work."

Leigh fluttered her eyelashes at him, feigning innocence. "Who, me? I'm not up to anything. How could I be with you and Nathan and Trent on me every second of every day? I'm almost twenty-two, Chase."

"Spare me the melodrama. Just because I don't want my baby sister having wild sex in a classic Trans Am in front of my house doesn't make me a meddler."

Leigh snorted loud enough to make some of the ladies in the row in front of them turn to see what was happening. But Leigh, as usual, ignored everyone around her and barreled on.

"If it were up to my brothers, I'd still be a virgin,"

she actually hissed at him. "Thank goodness I decided to go away for college. No one in Austin has ever heard of the Barrett brothers."

Chase opened his mouth to say something but ended up gaping at his sister like a dead fish. He was still formulating what to say to Leigh's pronouncement when Megan started her presentation.

Good manners, drilled into him over the years, forced him to remain silent and listen to the speaker. But what in the blue bejesus was up with the women tonight? And why was he the lucky man who got to be trapped in the middle of it?

And since when wasn't Leigh a virgin? He glanced at his sister, who was nodding and smiling at Megan as she went over the reasons why the city park needed new playground equipment.

He had to face facts. Their father had run off with a waitress when Leigh had been four. Their mother had died when Leigh had been eleven. She'd been raised by three older brothers who might have been strict with her but who did a fair amount of hell-raising on their own.

He should count his lucky stars that Leigh hadn't made him an uncle already.

But for crying out loud. He was all for liberated women, but did they all have to liberate themselves in front of him at the same time?

He turned away from Leigh, but not before making a mental note to talk to her once more about safe sex and nice boys.

Behind him, Chase could actually feel Janet Defries staring at the back of his head. No doubt she was planning all the things she could do to him if she had plastic wrap and an economy jar of mayonnaise.

And then there was Megan. Frowning, he looked at her. She was carefully explaining how the city could build a large play castle like so many bigger cities had if they raised enough money and had enough volunteers.

Her talk was going well, as expected, but Chase could tell she was nervous. They'd been friends for so long, he recognized the signs.

He gave her an encouraging smile.

And the look she gave back scorched him. Good Lord. She was picturing him naked.

Before he could stop himself, before he could even think about how downright stupid it was, he found himself picturing Megan naked, too.

And really, really liking what he pictured. Sure, a few times over the years, he'd turned the idea of Megan over in his mind. After all, she was attractive in a sedate sort of way.

She had long ash-blond hair, pretty green eyes, and a slim body with just enough curves to keep a man interested. Sweet curves that would be soft to the touch, and silky to the taste and—

Whoa. What in the blazes was he doing? Megan Kendall was one of his best friends, not to mention a woman who actually believed in things like love and marriage. He blinked and mentally tossed a thick, woolen blanket over Megan's naked body. That would be the end of that.

"I think Chase should co-chair the committee with Megan," Leigh announced, bringing Chase's attention back to the meeting going on around him.

He glared at Leigh. "What? I don't have time to co-chair a committee." He glanced at the city council, the mayor, and finally, at Megan. "Sorry. I'm too busy at the moment."

"Everyone is busy," Earl said. "But you make time for something as important as this." The mayor leaned forward. "Don't you want your children to have a nice park to play in someday, Chase?"

"I don't have any children, Earl, and I don't plan on having any."

He looked at Megan, whose expression could only be called sad. Great. Just great. Now he'd disappointed her by saying he wouldn't co-chair the committee. Well, at least he'd found a way to get her to stop picturing him naked.

"Hold on a minute here," Leigh said. "It's your turn to help, Chase Barrett. Trent's the chief of police, so he does a lot for this town. And Nathan's computer company supports practically everybody. I've volunteered at the senior center, and I'm coming back to town next fall to do my student teaching. It's your turn to do something to help."

A slow, steady throbbing sensation started somewhere in the back of Chase's brain. Leave it to his sister to put him in an awkward position. "I don't have the time right now, Leigh. I'll be happy to make a donation, though."

Megan's expression softened. She forgave him. He knew she forgave him. Naturally, sweet Megan would understand.

Dang it. Now he felt lower than a rattlesnake's rump.

"What would it involve?" he half groaned, wanting to do whatever it took to get out of this room and away from these women.

"It wouldn't be much," Megan told him. "Just help with the carnival and the auction. I'd only need a couple hours of your time for the next few weeks."

Like he believed that. A carnival and an auction sounded like a lot of work. "Why do we have to have both?"

Leigh thwacked him on the arm. "Weren't you listening? Megan explained that the carnival will bring in the people, then the auction will bring in the big money."

Chase frowned at his sister. "Oh."

"I'll be willing to help on this committee if Chase is co-chair," Janet said from over his shoulder.

The throbbing in the back of his head grew more intense as several other single women in the room also agreed to help on the committee, that is of course, "if he did, too."

"See there, Chase, you're a popular guy. Lots of folks want to help out if you join in," Earl said. He glanced at the members of the city council. "I think this sounds like a great plan. Let's take a vote."

Chase wasn't surprised the council agreed with the mayor. What wasn't to like? Everyone was happy except for him.

"I never agreed to help," he pointed out to Leigh after Megan gathered her things and headed back to sit down.

"Oh, let it go, Chase. You're like a neutered hound

dog, going on about something that's long gone," Leigh said.

A soft, sexy, feminine laugh floated around him, raising his body temperature. Who in the world... He turned, bumping right into Megan. The smile she gave him was so very unlike the Megan he'd known for years and years.

Her smile was pure seduction.

"Trust me, Chase is nothing like a neutered hound dog," she said softly.

The water. Something was definitely wrong with the water in this town.

ALSO BY LORI WILDE & LIZ ALVIN

Handsome Devil Series:
Handsome Rancher
Handsome Lawman
Handsome Cowboy

ALSO BY Lori Wilde
Texas Rascals Series:
Keegan
Matt
Nick
Kurt
Tucker
Kael
Truman
Brodie
Dan
Rex
Clay
Jonah

ABOUT THE AUTHORS

Liz Alvin

Liz Alvin has loved reading and writing for as long as she can remember. In fact, she majored in literature at college just so she could spend her days reading great stories. When it came to her own stories, she decided to write romances with happy endings because she's a firm believer in love. She's been married to her own hero for over 30 years. They live in Texas near their adult children and are surrounded by rescue dogs and a rescue cat.

Lori Wilde

Lori Wilde is the New York Times, USA Today and Publishers' Weekly bestselling author of 88 works of romantic fiction. She's a three time Romance Writers' of America RITA finalist and has four times been nominated for Romantic Times Readers' Choice Award. She has won numerous other awards as well.

Her books have been translated into 26 languages, with more than four million copies of her books sold worldwide.

Her breakout novel, *The First Love Cookie Club*, has been optioned for a TV movie.

Lori is a registered nurse with a BSN from Texas

Christian University. She holds a certificate in forensics, and is also a certified yoga instructor.

A fifth generation Texan, Lori lives with her husband, Bill, in the Cutting Horse Capital of the World; where they run Epiphany Orchards, a writing/creativity retreat for the care and enrichment of the artistic soul.